PLANET OF GHOSTS
AND OTHER STORIES

WESLEY R. BISHOP

Denver, Colorado

Published in the United States by:

Spaceboy Books LLC
1627 Vine Street
Denver, CO 80206

www.readspaceboy.com

Text copyright ©2026 Wesley R. Bishop
Artwork copyright ©2026 Wesley R. Bishop
and Spaceboy Books LLC

Cover features CC0 and Public Domain assets.

All rights reserved. No portion of this book may be reproduced, copied, transmitted or stored at any time by any means mechanical, electronic, photocopying, recording or otherwise, without the prior, written permission of the publisher.

First printed March 2026

ISBN-13: 978-1-951393-53-3

Praise for **PLANET OF GHOSTS and OTHER STORIES:**

"Bishop writes with a rare blend of heart, wit, and sharp speculative clarity. *Planet of Ghosts and Other Stories* is a collection that lingers in the funny, unnerving, and sometimes quietly devastating ways only the best sci-fi can. These stories sift through the ruins of Earth and the complexities of human belief, asking what it means to carry memory forward. 'Walmart World Heritage Site' is one of my all-time favorite short stories: darkly hilarious, piercingly smart, and sneakily tender. I think about it constantly especially when I make my way to the cart corral. Bishop doesn't just imagine futures; he reanimates the absurdity, sorrow, and sacred detritus of our present."

— Mauve Perle Tahat, PhD, author of *Ecologies of Incarceration: Carceral Discard Studies in the Anthropocene* (2024) and *Spatial Residue: Plastic Affects and Configurations of Place* (2026)

"*Planet of Ghosts* is a searing examination of a dying Earth. Bishop's prose is reflective of what is seemingly right in front of us while simultaneously extending the depths of dystopian imagination. Through humor and heartbreak, the reader will journey into the desperate grips of a failing planet, but with the ultimate reminder that '[e]very problem humanity faces is always only one generation away from a solution.' Let this collection be your awakening."

— Kailey Tedesco, author of *MOTHERDEVIL*

Also by Wesley R. Bishop

An Atheist's Book of Prayers: Poems

A Migration of Cranes to a Temporary River: Poems

The Sound of Color: Poems

COVID19 HAIKU: Short Poems in a Long Year

The Digital Self: Poems and Illustrations

Liberating Fat Bodies:
Social Media Censorship and Body Size Activism
with Bessie Rigakos

Schoolhouse Stories
with Ken Williams and Roger Pickenpaugh

From the Hills of Southeastern Ohio with Ken Williams

My Poetics: Poems and Essays

To Steven: Poems
with Steven King

To Allison, always.

"Make yourself an ark of gopher wood, and place rooms in the ark, and cover it inside and out with pitch."

— Genesis, 6:14

TABLE OF CONTENTS

PART ONE

THE WAITING ROOM 1

PLANET OF GHOSTS 15

WALMART WORLD HERITAGE SITE 41

TWO BY TWO 51

THE DEPARTMENT OF REPAIR AND RECALL FOR ROBOTICS INDUSTRY 65

WILLIAM HOWARD TAFT IS CONFUSED BY TIME TRAVEL 68

TERMS AND CONDITIONS 73

PART TWO

PHARAOH'S TOMB 79

THE MAN WHO SAVED THE DEAD 114

LEG UP 131

LAUNCH PAD 146

SPARKY IS A GOOD BOY 150

HOPE SPRINGS 168

FLOOD WATERS 181

ACKNOWLEDGEMENTS 187

ABOUT THE AUTHOR 189

PART ONE

THE WAITING ROOM

God waited for the end of the universe. God had begun existence lonely, and God would end it the same way. Scanning the universe once more, God was not surprised to find no sentient being left to talk with. At this late hour in the universe, everything had shrunk down to the size of a galaxy. Within the next few moments, the entire universe would violently contract once more, this time to the size of a large solar system.

God tried once again to spread its awareness beyond the great mass collected on the horizon but could not. God had never been able to go beyond the universe. Even in the time of expansion, when the universe had raced outward, God had only been able to know what was on its side of existence.

Turning back to the sole remaining galaxy, God listened to the flowers that grew on a particular planet with no name. To attract herbivores, the flowers had evolved a curious organ in the interior of their petals. When the wind blew through them, they released a beautiful humming noise, bringing massive floating grazers who chomped on the flowers with their mouths. The floating grazers loved the flower and stems, but found the roots to be bitter, and therefore spit the roots back out as they sailed above the planet's orange-red fields. Scattered about, the roots began to regenerate into new flowers, and so the whole process was repeated.

Many times, God had taken the form of the floating grazers and sailed in their large herds, hunting the beautiful melodies.

But alas, in just a few moments the gentle grazers and delicate flowers would cease to exist. Suddenly the universe trembled again, more violent than it ever had before. God braced itself as all of existence began to contract.

God had not always gone without creatures to talk to. At the universe's height, it had been teeming with life forms that not only talked, but sang, screeched, wailed, honked, exploded, and chirped.

That was not to mean God was always successful in communicating with the other life forms in the universe, or that the conversations ever amounted to anything. Quite the contrary, most of the time the interactions resulted in disaster for the species in question.

One of the first species God tried to talk to was a fascinating race of intelligent, mobile rocks. The universe had been young in those days; God had been around for barely a trillion years, but it had grown bored from watching matter race away towards the horizon and seeing giant clouds of gas ignite and explode. So, when God had finally discovered another sentient being, God had been overjoyed with excitement.

Manifesting before a particular piece of slate, God began God's very first conversation.

"Hello," God said.

Startled, the piece of slate looked up from its meal of alkaline metals.

"Who said that?"

"It's me. I am me." God said. "What is your name?"

Of course, God already knew the answer to this question. Being God, God could trace every single one of the creature's atoms back to the creation of the universe. But God thought that showing off omniscience would be rude.

"They call me Grag," the piece of slate answered.

This whole conversation thing is easy. God thought.

Looking more closely at God, Grag asked what it had been wanting to know its entire existence. "So, the others were right? You do exist?"

"Uh..." God said. "I don't know what you mean."

"You are the All-Powerful Mountain, which sprang forth in the beginning to give life to all of us."

"Oh," God answered. "Well, not exactly. On your planet, the idea is popular that an All-Powerful Mountain gave birth to your people, but that isn't exactly what happened."

"I knew it!" Grag shouted. "The Pinnacle Rocks have been lying to us all these years."

"Well," God said, "I think they are honestly just mistaken."

"No," Grag insisted. "They shattered a piece of quartz last season for denying the existence of the Mountain."

"Yes," God said uncomfortably. "I saw that. But you know, what's done is done. You can't go back and change it."

"NO!" Grag yelled. "I will show the Pinnacle Rocks that they are mistaken. I will go to my people and tell them that you have blessed me with your truth. I will be your messenger, and I will— through your glory— spread the truth!"

With that, Grag turned away from God and began rolling as fast as it could.

"Wait!" God shouted after it. "Come back! I only wanted to talk with you! Maybe we could discuss the weather or something pleasant?"

But Grag would have no part of it. Every other member of the rock species that God spoke to reacted in the same way, until the entire race was at war with one another. Horrified, God watched as the first intelligent species destroyed itself. Years after God's first encounter God witnessed the final rock creature killing its last enemy. As it lay shattered before its base, God once again materialized on the planet.

"What have you done?" God asked.

"Oh, Crystalline Savior! The struggle is finally over, the non-believers have been vanquished. Glory to the All-Powerful Mountain! I am ready to reap my rewards."

"Reward!?" God exclaimed. "Why would I give you a reward? You just murdered the second to the last of your kind."

"But it is written that once the non-believers are destroyed, you will come back and take all that are faithful, polish them, and set them in the heavens to shine down for eternity."

Following its gaze God looked up at the stars.

"Don't you get it?" God pleaded. "There is no eternity with me. Once you die the material you are made of moves to a different state in the universe. That's all that happens. How can I take you anywhere but here? You couldn't survive on any of the other planets but this one. Where do you want me to take you? A nebula? What would you stand on? Or a frozen moon? Without an atmosphere of helium, you would suffocate."

God finished speaking and sat down in frustration.

"If you are not here to reward me, then what shall we do?"

"Well," God said looking up in hope, "maybe we could just talk?"

The last rock creature looked at God for a moment and then started to laugh.

"I see, you are not the true All-Powerful Mountain, but are instead the Dark Ravine's messenger sent to test my resolve. Very good trickster, but you will not fool me. I will remain dedicated to the Crystalline Savior until it rewards me with my immortality."

With that, God vanished from the planet, never to return.

+++

God gazed at the universe once more. The violent contracting had ceased for the moment, but it was only a matter of time before it started again. The next time would probably be the last.

The cosmos had been concentrated on the rim of existence, but as it had shrunk, there was now not enough room. Bits of planets and rocks hurtled through burning stars. Comets and balls of gas, previously separated by light years, were side by side. Black holes, no longer isolated in space, were violently sucking everything towards them.

Materializing on one of the few intact planets, God looked up at the sky in wonder. God had chosen a female Ipswitch to inhabit, mostly because their sense of sight had been unparalleled in the universe. Training her seven eyes on the heavens she watched as millions of objects whizzed by.

Materializing on the surface of an oncoming black hole, God chose the form of a male Spobler, mostly because their sense of sound was exhilarating. Every noise the giant ears picked up created an explosion of color in God's temporary brain.

Slam, crimson; *Crash*, yellow; *Boom*; violet!

Staring at the black hole, her Ipswitch eyes spotted the Spobler.

Straining his Spobler ears, he heard the planet begin to break apart.

Then God appeared between the two forms of itself as a Zezir. Their species were fascinating. They took the noises and sights of the universe and turned them into elaborate interstellar dances. At the species height, they had been one of the most populous in the universe, dancing in the void of worlds. God had often wondered who they danced for, since God and passing comets were the only beings who ever saw them.

Awesome images of destruction danced in her Ipswitch eyes. Terrifying sounds lit up all hemispheres of his Spobler brain. Their Zezir plasma limbs twisted, listening, and corkscrewing in ways that communicated the slow loss of space in an infinite loop.

And then it was over. The forms were destroyed, and God was returned to God's formless self.

God thought about creating a pair of lungs so God could sigh a breath of despair, or a pair of eyes to sob, but decided against it. Nothing would change God's feeling of hopelessness.

God was going through one of the most terrifying experiences a life form could witness and had no one to comfort God.

But this had been the story of God all along. No form was ever able to fully understand God. Even the ones that did not destroy themselves were unable to satisfy God's desire for camaraderie.

But as everything was being destroyed, God could not help but want someone to talk with. And not only talk, but also listen and understand what God was going through.

As God had done so many times before, each time proving to be unsatisfying, God decided to give it one more try. Concentrating all of God's power, God duplicated.

"Hello," God said to God.
"Hello," answered God.

"This is absolutely terrifying," God observed.

"Tell me about it."

"I would, but you already know everything I'm going to say."

"Right."

Both Gods said nothing for a few moments and awkwardly watched a star go supernova in an area the size of a small moon.

"So," God said finally breaking the silence. "Do you really think that we will cease to exist when the universe is done contracting?"

"I do," God answered. "Or at least we will cease to exist in our present forms. I can't fathom that we will be able to survive in that small of a space."

"Terrifying," God said.

"Tell me about it," God replied.

"I would but you... well you know."

"Right."

Again, the two became silent.

"You know what we need," God finally said.

"What?"

"We need a Centapadial."

"Funny, I was just thinking that."

"I know," God answered.

The Centapadials had been one of the few creatures in the universe that had not destroyed themselves once God spoke to them. Long, slender, and delicate, the Centapadials had possessed elongated brains that made them extremely intelligent. For thousands of years, they crawled about their planet living peaceful lives. They never evolved appendages that could manipulate their environments, so they never invented cities. And since they never invented cities, they never needed to have governments to organize them. And since they never invented governments, they never needed weapons to gain more power for those governments.

They were just highly intelligent creatures that enjoyed exploring their world and talking with one another.

God had spent many centuries on the Centapadials world, crawling with them, and having discussions. Eventually, though, the Centapadials had died out. A fungus on their world had evolved into a deadly spore that infected the Centapadials' brains, and slowly rotted them from the inside out. Watching them perish by the millions, God offered to help. The few remaining Centapadials had listened to God's offer, and after some consideration decided against accepting the divine intervention.

"You have been an interesting acquaintance," one of the Centapadials said as they slowly died. "But our time in the cosmos is done. Everything must come to an end at some time."

"But you have been one of the best companions that I have ever met."

"Unfortunately, my dear friend, you have no true companions. You are one of a kind, and just as it is our nature to exist, then disappear, it is your nature to continue existing alone."

With that the Centapadial slumped over and succumbed to the fungus raging through their body.

Unable to watch such magnificent creatures continue to suffer God left the world. Eons later God gave into temptation and tried to create new Centapadials, but eventually their sound reasoning always arrived at the same conclusion: they should not be in the universe anymore and God should accept God's fate.

During these final moments of the universe, however, God did not care. God simply wanted someone to talk to in the hopes of calming the rising panic.

"Okay," God said. "You concentrate on creating a solid place for them to crawl. I'll make a breathable atmosphere."

"Alright," God said once finished. "Now you protect it from any other objects."

"Already done," God replied. Both watched as an entire asteroid belt bounced off the protective newly created barrier.

"Good, keep that up and I will make the Centapadial."

Concentrating God created the Centapadial. Bursting into existence the new companion began to crawl back and forth on its planetary aquarium.

"Hello," God said. "How are you?"

"I...I don't know," the Centapadial answered. "I was just created for artificial conversation. How should I be? Since you created me, you would have a better understanding of that than me."

"See," God said to God. "Nothing like the clarity of a Centapadial's thoughts."

Ignoring God, God answered the Centapadial.

"You should probably be terrified."

"Oh. And why is that?"

"Because the universe and everything in it is about to be destroyed."

"Will it be painful?"

"Most likely, yes," both Gods answered.

"I see. Well then to answer your original question — I am terrified."

All three creatures sat quietly for a few moments. Finally, one of the Gods spoke.

"This really isn't all that comforting."

"I didn't think it would be," God replied.

"Sorry," the Centapadial answered. "Is there any way I can help?"

"Not really," both Gods answered.

"Well then what should we do?"

"We'll just have to wait," the Gods echoed.

"Will waiting help ease our fear?"

"Actually," God said as God began to think, "there was one creature I remember who could make waiting for something very monotonous." Looking at the other God, God asked, "Do you remember the humans?"

"Yes, of course I do."

"And do you remember their waiting rooms?"

"Yes."

"Well, let's create a waiting room and a human to go along with it. I always marveled how humans took horrible situations and blunted it with boredom."

"Do we have anything to lose?" The Centapadial asked.

"Not really," both Gods answered.

"Then we should give it a try."

"Clear Centapadial thinking," God said to God. "Nothing like it in the universe."

"Okay," God said. "Here goes."

Just as God was about to create the waiting room and the human, the universe shuddered so violently that God felt space and time begin to tear.

"Help!" The Centapadial shouted, but it was too late. The force of the universe tore the safe habitat to bits and thrust both Gods closer together.

"Oh no," God said to God.

All around them matter had ceased to retain any meaningful form. Mass became energy only to condense back into mass. Light radiated and ricocheted to and fro in terrible bursts of heat.

"I don't think there is enough room for the both of us," God said.

"I agree."

And with that the two Gods became one once again.

Alone, God began to panic.

Make it stop! God thought as the universe pushed in even tighter. *Please!*

For the first time in its existence God wished there were a higher being in the universe, one that could hear its prayers. But nothing came.

Staring at the center of the universe, feeling the walls of existence closing in, God tried to push existence back. Nothing happened.

The most terrifying thought racing through God's mind was not that it was about to die, that at least would have an ending, but that the whole thing was just getting ready to start all over.

It didn't take a Centapadial's rationality to figure out that God had once came into the cosmos ignorant of everything in existence, and that this beginning had probably been prefaced with a similar destruction of the universe. If it had happened once, it had happened before that, and before that, and before that. An eternity of being born, existing, violently dying, only to repeat the whole process again.

God wanted out. It couldn't contemplate spending another eternity watching other creatures live, love, laugh, and die. God was horrified at the prospect of being stuck in a never-ending story, a continuous loop.

Can anyone hear me! God thought with all of its might. *Can anyone help me!*

In response, the universe gave its final shudder.

NO! God thought.

In one single moment, all of existence occupied a speck of dust. It had done this countless times before. It would do so countless times again.

Just as the whole of existence was beginning to feel comfortable in its tight quarters something awoke. With a tiny nudge, God sent the entire universe into a violent explosion. Racing along at the front of the spreading wave, God marveled at what it was seeing. In all directions, it watched as the universe expanded and disappeared into space and time.

Fascinating, God thought.

Silent for what seemed millennia, God watched a beautiful nebula take form and light up with explosions. Gliding through the universe it saw stars spark and begin to burn, planets violently slam into one another, only to reform later. After roughly a billion years, God began to feel lonely.

Curiously, God began to look for someone, anyone, to speak with.

PLANET OF GHOSTS

At first when the colonists arrived on the planet, they did not notice the ghosts. Sleeping in their pods on the massive desert, the first ghost they saw was their former engineer, Haruko Jones. She had died in flight to the new planet, and at first, people thought it was just nightmares. After all, the death of Haruko had been traumatic for all onboard. They had come out of their sleep cycle— one of the thirteen planned during the trek— and during a maintenance check Haruko had been smashed by a faulty bulkhead.

Nearly two dozen of the one hundred and fifty onboard had seen the incident, and word quickly spread throughout the ship.

"It was awful," one passenger, a young woman named Ava, said to her polycule as they nestled back into their pod for another cryo-sleep cycle. "She was just standing there with her wrench, and then..."

"Don't think about it. Next sleep cycle will last several centuries. Just think of it this way, she belongs to the dead now, like those back on Earth," one of the partners, Henry, a big burly man with a black beard said.

"By the time we wake back up, she would have been thousands of years old," the other partner, a short ginger man named Michael, added.

"You're right." The three shared a small kiss and then went back to sleep.

But now they were on the planet, this new planet of rocks and desert and sparse vegetation. A planet that did not have a name but just a number. People were finding it impossible to forget Haruko Jones. The first night the colonists thought they were dreaming individually, and as they broke out the supplies the next morning, no one made much comment about their assumed nightmares. But by the fifth night, one of the medics said they kept dreaming about the dead engineer, and then slowly, people began to talk.

"I saw her too."

"Me too. Out by the rocks at the edge of camp."

"Wait, you actually saw her, here? Or saw her in a dream?"

It was discovered, after a quick round of interviews with the ship's three-person counseling team, that nearly everyone was seeing Haruko. As the nights wore on, the sightings spread until every single one of the passengers was reporting seeing her ghostly figure out among the rocks.

"What do you see when you see her in the rocks?" A counselor asked a witness.

"Just her, with her wrench, trying to make repairs."

"Does she say anything?"

"Yeah, she keeps saying 'Are we there? Have we made it?' and then she smacks her wrench against the rocks. It's like she is frustrated but doesn't know it."

The counselor made notes. That night she saw the same thing.

Word spread again. Quickly, people not only saw her, but began to hear the same thing. And so, for several nights, the dreams of the crew of the *Gem City* were filled with the voice of Haruko Jones, the dead engineer, questioning the desert.

"Are we there?"

BANG.

Have we made it?

BANG

"Are we there?"

BANG.

On and on it went for nearly two weeks, until finally someone awoke one morning and said they had not seen Haruko, but someone else. "He was standing there! Just like he looked on Earth," the woman told a counselor.

"Who?"

"My son, Ilhan. Only, that is impossible, he died in an accident before we even left Earth. Before we had even decided to come here!"

"What was he doing?" the counselor asked.

"Nothing. Just looking for food, he was always such a hungry boy, looking for food and wandering among the rocks."

And, just as with Haruko, the woman's son Ilhan quickly spread in the visions of the colonists. The *Gem City*'s chief scientist, Beatrice Caddel, led repeated expeditions into the fields of towering rocks but found nothing.

"I honestly don't know what's happening," she told Captain Jothen. "The rocks all range in size and composition, which is odd, but the minerals are not toxic... at least there's nothing to indicate they are toxic..."

"Then why am I seeing my dead wife?" Jothen asked. She had seen her for three nights in a row. Wandering among the rocks asking the void if she was going to pull through the sickness? Her hair was as lovely as ever. She didn't tell anyone this, but that's what shocked Jothen. Even here millennia later, under an alien sky, her wife's hair found a way to glow with that red gold Jothen had first fallen in love with.

"It could be anything," Caddel continued. "Radiation from this sun, the minerals in the soil, particulates in the air... for all we know we could have changed in our voyage here. Humans living for thousands and thousands of years... maybe that's it? Maybe it's a development in us? When we go to sleep each night in the pods, it's like we are deep sleeping again in space... maybe we could try sleeping outside of them?"

"But why would that matter?" Jothen asked.

"I don't know; it's just a guess and worth a try. I cannot..." Caddel paused. "I just can't spend each night like this."

"Anything is worth a try," Jothen agreed. She was getting weary too. One evening her new partner, Carol, had to hold her back as she tried following the ghost of her former wife into the rocks.

"Don't do it," Carol had told Jothen.

"Why? I need to see if these ghosts pose a risk to us." And, Jothen didn't add, she was mesmerized at how her hair shun in the moon's light.

"Please don't leave me," Carol asked again. They had met on one of the awakenings during the voyage, the one after Haruko had died. Everyone was on edge. Jothen had just finished her inspection of the crew and ship, and just as she was about to climb back into her pod, Carol had asked if she could join her. The two had been inseparable since.

"What's wrong? What do you see?" Jothen asked.

"I just don't want to be left alone listening to my old husband," Carol said as she pulled closer to Jothen's chest. Slowly, as if Carol were sharing a memory, the ghost of Carol's husband appeared. But it was odd. The ghost was a shifting mass... almost as if he were trying to decide what shape his face was like. "What did your ex-husband look like?" Jothen asked Carol. "Like... well..." Carol pulled her pad from its charging station and retrieved an image of him. Sure enough, as soon as Jothen saw the image, the ghost in front of her solidified, his features settling like a piece of drying clay.

"You... you were married to him?" Jothen asked.

"Yes, and I don't want to talk about it," Carol answered.

The crew and passengers of the *Gem City* did begin to follow the ghosts into the rock fields, and as they did, they began to suspect that the chief scientist's hypothesis was correct. It was not the new environment. At least not totally. Something was happening to them. They were sharing their thoughts, their memories. The ghosts were a contagion of memory. One evening as a group neared Haruko, the air seemed to shift, and the ghost disappeared only to reappear a few feet away and resume banging on the rocks.

The group looked on in a mixture of wonder and terror.

"People, people!" Jothen spoke the next day above the panicked chatter of the colonists. Jothen was concerned, not just due to "the sharing" that was spreading at a greater and greater rate, but that if left unchecked much longer, the situation would go from a mixture of fear to full-fledged panic. The ship's passengers were supposed to be setting up a colony, determining elections, finding places to grow crops. They were not supposed to be chasing ghosts in fields of rocks.

"I have an idea," the ship's historian, DeShawnda Robinson, offered. "But it may not work."

Jothen and the colonists looked at her in earnest.

"Please Dr. Robinson, anything at this point is worth trying," Jothen said.

"Well... see, on Earth some cultures built what were called 'Spirit Houses.' The idea was that if you built a place for the spirit to live it would choose to stay there and not haunt your home."

Caddel rolled her eyes. "But there is no reason to believe these are actual spirits. All the evidence points to us; we are conjuring up these visions. The problem is psychological, or... I don't know... maybe in the atmosphere.... I just know it's not supernatural."

"Maybe," DeShawnda admitted, "but we could try building one of these spirit houses and see if we can compel the spirit to live there and not wander among the rocks. As you say Beatrice," and with this DeShawnda looked at Caddel coldly, "this is all just in our heads. Maybe if we picture putting these spirits in a place, they will stay there. It's just an idea, though."

"But that leaves the issue," Carol spoke up, "of figuring out how we are going to build all of these spirt houses. Where are we going to find the materials?"

Jothen placed her hand on one of the rocks. They were everywhere, and for the most part soft like sandstone.

"I have an idea," Jothen said.

And so, all that day a small group worked on fashioning one of the rocks into a small home. They hollowed out the rock so that a single person could enter and sit. They finished just as the planet completed its day rotation and night fell.

"Alright," one of the colonists, a young woman named Hawker, said. "Now what?"

Already the landscape was filling with all manner of ghosts. Hawker had been a refugee who had joined the *Gem City* group after their initial charter had been approved. Jothen believed Hawker came from the remnants of Indianapolis. The mere mention of the city made Jothen shudder.

The stories had not been pretty about the conditions of the city-state in the years leading up to their departure. It was why no one was surprised that Hawker's ghosts were militia members yelling as they fired madly into the air.

"Alright," Jothen said. "Everyone imagine Haruko Jones." Hawker and the other colonists turned to Jothen. As they did, she appeared, Haruko, wrench in hand, banging on the rocks.

"Engineer Jones," Jothen commanded. Haruko turned, her face pale and blank. "This is your new home. You will be staying here from now on. Haruko looked at her wrench, then at the rock.

"Are we there?" Haruko asked as she walked into the center of the rock. "Have we made it?"

With that she sat down on the small bench and fell silent. Everyone watched in amazement.

"But what if someone conjures her out?" Hawker wondered.

"Why would anyone do that?" Carol asked.

"Yes, indeed they shouldn't," DeShawnda added. "To work we should be committed, collectively, to keeping the ghosts in these rock houses."

The colonists, bolstered by the success of this initial experiment, attempted other methods too. They tried ordering the ghosts to walk towards the horizon, and not come back. But it didn't work as the ghosts seemed to get distracted as they walked and ended up making more noise than before. The colonists also tried telling the ghosts to just stay by a rock, but again it was almost as if the lack of ceremony did something to them. They would stand at the unaltered rock for only an hour or so, sometimes most of the evening, but would eventually start wandering again. Only when the spirit house was made, and the ghost ordered in, did the apparition stop wandering and making noise.

Even though it took away valuable labor power, Jothen created a special group to start systematically making these spirit homes in the countless rocks in the desert. Occasionally, the crews came across such a large rock that they could make several seats. These spirit houses could house a dozen, sometimes more. The largest, which the colonists nicknamed "The Citadel" could house nearly a hundred ghosts. After about six months, it seemed as if the colonists had finally run out of ghosts. Jothen had made the decision to limit the spirit houses to a specific direction. She did not want the new colony ringed by houses for the dead, and so the spirit houses stretched south from the main camp and ran for almost five kilometers. To the north, east, and west, the colonists left open the land for planting and their building projects.

They all wondered, especially DeShawnda, what would happen in a few decades when the first generation of colonists slowly passed onto the next generation, and the truth was, no one knew. Could a spirit house be used more than once? They found an answer to this when Ilhan's mother died unexpectedly one evening. She had been working with a crew when one of the lasers slipped in its machine holster and sliced through her. That night, of course, she appeared screaming in the desert about the burn.

Screaming how she, all of them really, had been forced from the Earth due to war, climate change, bigotry. Screaming that she simply wanted to go home with her son.

Jothen had the body moved to the spirit house of her son and buried there. Then as they had done countless times before, they deposited the spirit of the woman into the structure. What the colonists noticed was interesting. Ilhan was still there, but he was faint. It was as if his mother had replaced his luminescence. She shone brighter, like a moon outpacing a star in late evening.

DeShawnda set up camp near the structure and did research over several nights.

In two weeks, she reported her findings to Jothen.

"The ghosts do fade!" DeShawnda said.

Jothen was looking at her planner in the colony's main building. She was in the midst of figuring out the layout for the hospital. Originally, it was thought to place it in the center of the colony, but the more the colonists planned, the more it made sense to place it in the south. That way as colonists died their bodies and spirits could easily be transported into the spirit house district.

Jothen was fairly distracted on that day. Carol had decided to move out of their shared living space. Jothen could be wrong, but she imagined Hawker had caught her eye. Hawker was nothing if not gorgeous. She had dark hair that she kept buzzed on the sides, and on top the hair she did have flipped up in a celebratory and "fuck you" vibe. Plus, her arms were like chiseled rock. She was a natural soldier and fighter, something that made her survival in Illinois among militias not just plausible but destined. She was quickly rising as one of the needed leaders of their group.

As such, Jothen was readjusting to the single life.

Perhaps for the best.

She was captain after all, and there was still so much to do.

"Captain?" DeShawnda said again.

"They fade?" Jothen asked DeShawnda as she looked up from the plans. "What do you mean?"

"Come with me."

Jothen sat with DeShawnda outside of the spirit house and waited quietly. As the sun set, she could begin to hear the screams of Ilhan's mother.

"Look," DeShawnda pointed. Sure, Ilhan was far fainter, so much so that when Jothen did not look closely he disappeared entirely.

"My theory," DeShawnda said, "is that when the original person who remembers dies, the memory gets faint. Eventually, we won't be able to see Ilhan because no one will actually remember him."

"So... we shouldn't mark the graves?" Jothen wondered.

"No! I think it is vital we do. Each spirit house needs to have a record of who is dwelling there. Otherwise, we could get periodic waves of hauntings as people rediscover their ancestors and the dead. By forcing the ghosts to be here, in one spot, and then allowing people to conjure them at will, we can contain them, and over time, they will just fade. And we can assign areas for certain families, different figures, etc. Here," DeShawnda explained, "I have thought up some plans."

Pulling out her planner, DeShawnda showed Jothen what she had been thinking.

At the next colony meeting, Jothen introduced DeShawnda's concept.

"Wait," one of the other colonists asked, a medical doctor named Kendal. "So, these ghosts are actually just tied to our memories?"

"In a manner of speaking," DeShawnda said. "It's our individual memories, but we can collectively share them. But because of whatever phenomena is happening on this planet it makes those memories appear as visible phenomena."

The colonists discussed the possibilities of just forcing forgetfulness on everyone, but it was quickly realized that it was simply not feasible. Unless the colony destroyed the records of each of the deceased, and medically found a way to erase the memory of people from the colonists the ghosts would still appear as people lived their lives and died on the planet. Then, without any knowledge of what was happening, the colony would go through the whole process again and again.

It was only through putting the ghosts in spirit homes and leaving them there could the past exist in a contained space.

It was settled that DeShawnda's project would go forward. The colonists were simply tired of the business of ghosts and wanted to move onto happier topics. With Ilhan's mother dead, the colony was allowing a new colonist to be born. Eventually, the colonists would be free to reproduce at will, but for the first two years, it had been decided to keep the colony's population at its original number. That way it could be determined how many people the new habitat could feasibly support. The polyamorous group of three partners were selected via lottery to have the new child, and the colonists quickly moved to celebrating the new life, in this new home, and put the matter of ghosts behind them.

Jothen gave DeShawnda full range to continue her work. Three colonists were assigned to her, the ship's counselors, and they broke off from the main meeting to begin planning. As Jothen watched DeShawnda give instructions to the new members... initiates really... she could not help but wonder if they would eventually form the basis of a new religion here?

It felt like it.

They had left Earth, launched themselves into space from Dayton, Ohio's airfield, to flee the numerous turmoils of Earth. Jothen wanted to try to prevent as many of those problems from following them here. New start. New civilization. Do not bring the baggage of Earth, especially North America, to a new planet.

There was little way to get ahold of Earth now, but Jothen could not help but wonder— had the remaining ship builders and potential colonists finally been able to convince the zealots of the old planet to stop killing it? One group in North America had been notorious for holding back efforts to save the environment, end the sectarian violence, and imagine a better future.

Had they survived? Finally come to realize the exodus of ships were the best bet for humans?

It was all a matter of speculation now. How one answered depended on how much faith one had in humanity.

So, faith. There it was. Jothen wondered what type of religion would take hold in the culture of ghost houses they were building here?

The next day, the polycule went to the hospital and submitted their DNA to begin the process. The new child would take three months to develop, and once that was complete, they could take the child back to their homes as a family. In the meantime, they would start visiting Kendal weekly to bond with the child and start parenting classes.

"Think about how beautiful they'll be!" Ava said to her two partners. "I think our child is going to have my eyes... maybe... what do you think? Maybe your red hair, Michael!"

The three could see the child developing in the pod and talked about the various features that may or may not appear. They also talked about how exciting it would be to see the child grow up in this new world. The first human in their group was born off-Earth.

"What should we name them?" Henry asked.

"Oh, I know," Ava said. "Haruko."

The colony continued for the next several months without much incident.

DeShawnda continued her research and work. Eventually, she even had a structure made at the southernmost tip of New Gem City (the name the colonists had voted on). There she and her aids settled into study and discussed the best practices of taking care of the ghosts. The colonists had even started calling it the "Memory Institute." Jothen was elected governor of the new city, easily beating her opponent, Beatrice Caddel.

Things were starting to be what the colonists had expected, even with the ghosts and spirt house project.

That is until a little after the first year of the colonist's arrival.

About two dozen residents of New Gem City wanted to hold a parade commemorating the establishment of their new home. Obviously, this brought up discussions of what they were celebrating exactly? After all, it was not as if they had come here under happy pretense. They were refugees. Survivors. Would such an event bring up memories?

Opposition to the proposal gained some traction, but it was small. Climate catastrophe, overmining of the subterrain earth, wars of every variety. Did anyone want to run the risk of creating an event that would unleash the dead victims en masse of those events? There were those who thought the best way to survive was to download oneself into a computer. Entire digital colonies and satellites and cities of computers sprang up. And, of course, there were the time travelers, both those leaving their time to go to the past to save others, and those arriving from different futures to save their timeline.

And then there were the generational spaceships designed to flee Earth. The ships that had developed on Earth were of multiple kinds. Some were religiously affiliated, others with political similarities, and a great number more just democratic communities that came together to survive.

Gem City was exactly that type of ship. It had originated from the American Midwest in Dayton (known during the era of American nationalism as, of course, the Gem City). Dayton had been home to a massive military airfield, and several generational ships were constructed and launched from it. By the time *The Gem City* was proposed, so many wars and uprisings had shaken the former nations of Earth that this group, made mostly of Toronto, Chicago, and Detroit refugees, were eager to simply leave. They all shared a similar trauma of the border wars the former United States had initiated. Religious persecution was common too. Jothen remembered being chased out of the military for her sexuality and transition. The community of *Gem City* figured that this shared fleeing would be enough to bind them together.

What they had not planned on, however, was how the previous eras would haunt them. Would their memories be partisan, like the battles of Earth?

DeShawnda warned at a local meeting that the entire venture was too risky.

She was by this point well respected, but there was a wariness in the colony to fully give her sway over debates. Her team would accompany the survivors into the fields of rocks and help with the departed ghosts. That was fine. But the proximity to death was unsettling.

Also, the Memory Institute had developed all manner of rules and quasi rituals to help the survivors place the ghost in its structure. This, DeShawnda argued, was to ensure ghosts remained where they were placed.

The staff of the Memory Institute had even taken to wearing white robed shawls. It kept them warm and made them easily visible as they did their rounds in the spirit houses. There was even a member of DeShawnda's team who rode a quiet hover bike through the spirit houses at night seeing the luminescent ghosts peering back. When Jothen could see the rider, they looked like some figure from an old fable making the rounds for the dead in a cemetery.

"It's a mistake," DeShawnda said at the monthly meeting. "Conjuring those kinds of memories like that would be inviting chaos."

"Oh, here comes the high and mighty priestess with her decrees," Caddel commented. "Tell us, are you still the colony's historian or are you just a full-on priest now?"

Jothen sighed. Here came the fight again.

Caddel continued. "Are you going to start telling us DeShawnda what we can and can't do with our memories now? Hmm. Sounds an awful lot like what we escaped from Earth."

Jothen looked to the back of the meeting room where currently the only child of the colony, young Haruko was toddling about.

Hawker stood with Carol holding her hand watching them. She knew they were both on the list to have a child. If the food supply held up, which there was no reason it shouldn't, family planning could start in the next few months. Jothen made a mental note to herself, though, set up rotation for watching children during meetings. It was not right to have the same people isolated from the decision making because of childcare.

This community shouldn't operate like Earth... so much to do, Jothen thought. *So much to unlearn to start over right.*

Murmuring began in the meeting of colonists. Jothen brought her attention back to the front of the room. There was a growing consensus that the ghost project, and DeShawnda in particular, was gaining too much power.

The story that religious strife was to blame for Earth's destruction had been popular even before *The Gem City* had started construction. Jothen had always been skeptical of that. There had been plenty of times in human history when different religions co-existed peacefully. Blaming religion for the collapse of Earth just seemed too easy. Jothen believed there had been a cornucopia of shit that killed Earth.

Nonetheless, the new "priests" as they were sometimes called were easy targets.

"Governor?" DeShawnda asked Jothen. "What do you think about this proposed Memory Day?"

"Oh! Is the government going to tell us what we can and can't celebrate?" Caddel looked at Jothen and then the rest of the colonists. "Don't you see what is happening here? A new religion and a new government deciding things for us!"

Jothen sighed again.

The chief scientist had not only run for the governorship but also had launched a recall vote a month in when the colony had decided to move resources in ghost study to DeShawnda and away from Beatrice. The recall had failed, but having this kind of division was not good.

"No," Jothen said, interrupting Caddel before she could continue. "We will hold a vote. A simple majority will decide if the resources can go to this celebration. Regardless of what the majority decides, folks will be able to individually determine if they participate."

Jothen could see DeShawnda shaking her head in disapproval, her braided hair and white cloak swaying in disappointment.

"What did you want me to do DeShawnda? Beatrice to launch ANOTHER recall?"

"You are not responsible for her actions, but you are responsible for yours."

DeShawnda still had her back turned to Jothen. She was preparing her bike and lanterns. Apparently, tonight she had the rounds in the ghost houses.

Jothen hated when DeShawnda spoke like that.

Fuck. She was sounding more and more like a religious guru.

"We are facing another election in a year, and the community is still fragile. We cannot afford division." Jothen countered.

"Governor, there is always going to be a threat to us. Be we a colony, a city, or a planetary civilization." As in response to DeShawnda's point, Jothen began to imagine one of the many screaming politicians of her youth. The kind that was broadcast all over the world and who always seemed able to tap into whatever horrible disaster was happening and make it worse. She could almost feel, again, how those words against women, against religious minorities, against HER as she began to transition, had made her feel. It had been as if those words were radioactive and could burn just by hearing them.

"Jothen?" DeShawnda said.

Jothen blinked and refocused her attention on the community's historian. "Hmm?"

"That look, you were thinking about people from past Earth?"

Jothen didn't say anything.

"You've been lost in thought more than usual." DeShawnda handed her a tablet. "You can make an appointment if you would like to deposit whoever you were imagining later tonight. Beatrice's stunt of bringing up the religious persecution at the meeting has had folks in here making appointments all day. But we still have some slots. I'll accompany you personally if you'd like."

Jothen took the tablet and made an appointment. The later the better. She could sit in the waiting room of the Memory Institute and gather her thoughts while others dealt with their own ghosts and the memory day parade.

The Memory Day event went ahead. Most had voted for it, but only by a slim majority. This was opposed to the proposed recall vote Caddel called for, which lost in a landslide. The parade would take place in a week.

The day the festivities began, Caddel was leading the handful of colonists who had volunteered to recount the final recall vote (again). Once that was finished, they moved to the parade through the colony (really only four and half blocks at this point).

All seemed to go just fine during the day. People could, if they wanted, hold pictures of their loved ones up on their planners, and one by one, the ghosts of friends and family flicked into existence, walking beside the colonists.

That night, though, was a different story.

"DeShawnda," Jothen said in the doorway of the institute. Robinson was helping a colonist, one of the medical assistants, who was seeing a local preacher from Kentucky who had organized death squads.

Jothen had only caught the tail end of the conversation, so the ghost was half formed. He stood six feet away and yelled violently about "degenerates."

"Yes?" DeShawnda asked.

"Well... it's what you feared," Jothen said. Robinson's eyes closed. She could see the politician of the medic, plus her own ghosts following her about.

DeShawnda growled in frustration and followed Jothen out of the institute.

"This is going to take days, maybe weeks to clean up, Governor."

Jothen didn't say anything and instead rounded the corner, and in the city's center nearly the whole colony was present, gesturing wildly, staring at empty spaces. Some were even crying and holding one another.

DeShawnda had not attended the Memory Day events, so had no idea what was haunting everyone, out as she neared the small gazebo at the center, she caught the conversations. Talks of politicians, of militias, of lost family members. Like slow burning lights, the ghosts flickered into focus for DeShawnda and Jothen. Near the far end of the center, two groups of four or five colonists were bitterly arguing.

"That is not what happened at the Battle of Chicago!" one shouted. "They were heroes defending the city."

"They fired on refugees from Wisconsin," another said. "I saw it myself."

On cue two masses of ghosts appeared, one heroically defending the lawn with guns. Next to them were the same ghosts, but these laughed manically and fired their weapons into screaming masses of other ghosts. The scene played in an infinite loop.

"This is really, really not good," Jothen remarked.

DeShawnda stood quietly for a moment. "I've never seen such competing forms before."

"Hmm? What are you talking about?"

"The ghosts," she said pointing to the two differing militias. "Most ghosts, in fact almost all of the ones I've dealt with, are isolated. They are personal memories."

Jothen starred with DeShawnda for a moment. "Ah, well... that is fascinating... but could we maybe focus on the novelty of this later. Like after we have dealt with the crisis."

DeShawnda turned to Jothen. "Different people see different ghosts, and what is the only way you can see them?"

"Well, the easiest way is to tell someone what you are seeing."

"Exactly. And so, you could theoretically hold onto a memory forever, and no one would ever see the ghosts from it."

"Yes..." Jothen said. "But that would be horrible. Seeing them every night with no one to talk about it with. Who would want to do that?"

"Where's Beatrice?" DeShawnda said suddenly looking over the crowd of the colonists. At this point everyone, including the families with children, were present. The commotion of people's voices and the growing crowded din of ghost yells, screams, and sobs was making it impossible to discern any single voice. DeShawnda had no doubt that all of this had brought back memories of even ghosts laid to rest in the spirit houses.

"Caddel is in the gazebo," Jothen said.

DeShawnda made her way to the chief scientist, dodging wailing figures as she did. As she walked up the steps, Haruko Jones' ghost stepped in front of her.

"Are we there yet?" *BANG*. The side of the gazebo rang out in that eerie echo.

"Almost," DeShawnda assured, as she gently stepped aside from the deceased engineer. "Dr. Caddel? Beatrice? Where are you?"

The ghosts in the gazebo parted, and Beatrice sat with her knees pulled up to her chin.

"I suppose you are here to tell me 'I told you so,'" Beatrice said.

"No, I'm here for that," Jothen said. "DeShawnda is too big of a person for that. She's here to fix this"

"I'm here to tell you *I* was wrong," DeShawnda said.

Caddel and Jothen looked at her with surprise, then confusion.

"What do you mean?" Caddel asked.

"We were trying to just bury the dead here, put them out of sight and mind. Like it was some individual problem. But its more than that. There is a collective component too."

DeShawnda looked back at the warring, shifting masses of ghosts.

"What are you seeing, Beatrice?" DeShawnda asked. "What have you not shared with us?"

Beatrice looked away in shame. "I... I haven't told anyone... ever..."

Jothen began to understand. "It's alright. No one here should have to bear anything alone. Let's work on this together." Jothen finally allowed her eyes to move to the image of her late wife wandering around the grounds.

As Beatrice began to speak a new ghost began to appear.

"What happened?" DeShawnda asked.

And so, Beatrice Caddel recounted the story. It was traumatic. It was horrific. As Caddel spoke faster and faster, the shame and guilt she had been carrying whipped into phantoms about the three.

"No one is going to look at me the same way," Beatrice said drawing further into herself. "Jothen says it all the time. We are trying to build a better place here..."

"I am not so sure about that," Jothen said, looking again at the crowded colonists. "We are living here, but we haven't moved on... not really."

Sitting down, DeShawnda, Caddel, and Jothen talked through much. They talked about dead colleagues. Dead friends. All of them had killed to survive and make it to Dayton. Jothen talked about her wife, how hard it had been to get medicine.

The ghosts shifted like a light show, taking on the features of each memory and story.

Over the course of the night, others followed suit.

That evening sealed the colony's fate. New Gem City would succeed, and it would prosper. That night the first of many group sessions began. This was followed with group and individual therapy.

Although they were not aware of it, they had created the first holiday. Not a parade, but a night of memory, where people purposefully molded the ghosts with stories. As day broke, they walked as a community to the south and left the ghosts in their homes.

After a month from the first memory night, Jothen found herself walking into the field of spirit houses again. As her hand traced the stone, she thought of how they had brought much, left more, and still found the past waiting for them all this distance away from Earth. Somewhere in these living catacombs was the residual calls of a red-haired woman she had once loved so much. Jothen looked forward to seeing her and talking to her group about the experience. It was something not to flee, but to hold and acknowledge in pain's afterglow.

As Jothen walked back to her home, the sirens of New Gem City sounded. Immediately on high alert, Jothen ran to the security station.

"What is it?" she asked Hawker who was seated looking at the computer screens.

"You are not going to believe this," Hawker said. "There is another ship in orbit above us."

Jothen stared at the screen.

And so began the battle, the last battle of old Earth, between New Gem City and the ship *Pharaoh*.

TO BE CONTINUED...

WALMART WORLD HERITAGE SITE

Millennia after the destruction of Earth, and roughly forty generations removed from the original giant ships that left the dying planet, humans continue their returns to what remains so as to conduct archeological excavations.

What was left of Earth was strung across an asteroid belt, with larger chunks occasionally colliding with smaller pieces of the once blue green home.

Of course, the descendants had records of what had happened, but like all things there were questions left unanswered. This was the stuff that people, as they lived on the planet and fled to the stars, had not thought to write down. Or, as the case was with this mission, what the ancestors had left behind that needed closure.

Made more difficult for these archeologists was the fact that sites of memory were not systematically preserved. Instead, it was haphazard pieces of land atop floating, dead rock. In a few places, the atmosphere had been preserved, and there archeologists were able to see best how people had lived.

One of these sites was an ancient market named "Walmart."

The descendants of one vessel, the *Octavia*, were particularly interested in this area for what it contained buried under its ruins. Using their computers integrated into their minds centuries before, they could scan an area, upload any existing files from the tech of old Earth, and recreate what had occurred in a space.

As the archeologists disembarked their ship, the image of what had been took form. A blue vested man wearing the label *How Can I Help You?* greeted the archeologists.

Hello, the archeologists say. *We are well. How are you?*

The computer runs through the scenarios, and a host of options flood the archeologists' minds. The blue vested man smiles and says "Swell!" In another version, he waves and goes back to looking at his hand-held computer called "phone." This is all compiled by the surviving security footage, social media posts, the network *Octavia* was part of that contained sources on this period.

The archeologists had long ago given up the form of these ancestors, trading in legs and arms for tails and fins. Their bodies contained more helium than water, and as the digital recreation plays in their minds they float about the ruins.

Click, click, whoosh, one of the archeologists says. Letting out a bit of helium.

The other archeologists *click* in agreement.

Security footage is run through their minds, and they see their ancestors fighting over a flat screen computer called "television."

In another aisle, they watch as a child falls to the ground screaming. "I want it!!!!!!"

Click, click, and then a vertical roll of delight. The other archeologists follow suit, their way of laughing. One, the third lead on this mission, has children. They are prone to similar tantrums as well.

Ancient saying: *The More Things Change...* flashes through their computers.

The rolling stops when they get to a file marked: DISTURBING.

The archeologists upload it to their minds, and float to the area they believe was the site of the incident.

An ancestor appears in their field of vision. "Are you sure, archeologists, you wish to proceed? Warning is advised."

They mentally push past the warning and watch as the simulated ancestor pulls out a device, "gun," and begins to shoot wildly about. Other simulated ancestors scream and fall to the ground bleeding.

Click, click, screech. Helium fills the archeologists as they watch in distress. A debate ensues, old at this point in their profession, of whether they have a right to judge the past. Should they be here disturbing the dead?

The debate ends, as usual, in no set answer.

The archeologists begin to drift apart collecting data for their own specific projects.

One, a young archeologist on their first expedition, stares at a sign.

They make a note to focus on this for their future project. They scan the remaining structures below, "pipes," and recreate scenes where ancestors deposited their waste.

The third lead takes a large amount of helium into their body and floats high above the structure. They are looking for "office." Running through layout plans, and recreated footage, they finally find the century, then decade, then year they were searching for.

They upload the necessary files and listen.

This is five hundred years after the destruction of Earth. This market has been transformed from its original purpose to a site of history. Visiting travelers, still in bipedal form but already beginning to transition to flying beings, float about. Maps are stretched across one of the renovated walls depicting the rise and fall of the ancient commercial empires. The "Age of Walmart" is central and shows its expansion from the American South to the entire globe, highlighting the problems and benefits it brought to various people in uneven quantities, before collapsing in on itself as the display explains, "empires are bound to do."

Visitors, recreated by the archeologist, also learn about the Earth literary figures Danielle Steele (no relation to the tyrant of Saturn), and James Patterson (relation to the twenty-fourth century space explorer). There is even an exhibit talking about the early "phones." People coo and awe, blinking their eyes as they capturing pictures to upload to their virtual streams.

"Look everyone! We're at the Walmart World Heritage Site!"

The thoughts formed are released and slip into the collective consciousness of the archeologists.

In one area called "aisle" a visitor brags about how they and their partner have traveled to over twenty different World Heritage Sites. "Now, this is a great place and everything, definitely a symbol of culture, but if you really want to see something go to the Starbucks remains. It's one of the only ones left and they actually let you stand in line to get something to drink!"

A family from the generational ship *Toronto* (incidentally now a museum itself above Jupiter) nods their heads in interest. They release enough helium and settle on their feet, feeling the strange experience of weight solely supported by their legs.

"I mean, just think of it," they continue, "having to wait in line for something? It really made me think about how our ancestors had to live. *Absolutely amazing.*"

"Well," one of the *Toronto* visitors replies, "that really is something, but we just got back from the Chennai Memorial."

The woman stops and nods her head gravely. She produces helium in nervousness and rises a bit.

"They have the site set up so these invisible wires will play the voices of those who died in the attacks. It's really eerie. Kind of like walking through a garden of the dead. In fact, we saw them installing the new hologram feature when we were there. Soon you won't just hear what the people said on their phones during the attacks, but also the images that were captured. It will be just like you were there!"

In the aisle next to them, people look at the displays of "bar codes."

"This was a consumer society." The sign explains. "People of the past consumed to live, to enjoy, and to stabilize some of the specific national economies. As such, our ancestors here in the American Midwest, specifically, devised elaborate and sophisticated rituals to ship, display, and purchase goods. Our world heritage site is a testament to that history!"

The third archeologist speeds up the digital memories. Finally, they find the exact date they were looking for. They watch as an ancestor working at the world heritage site installs the wires that will feed the voices of the dead to visitors. The archeologist watches carefully and sees where they installed the ancient computer.

Click, click, roll to the right side. *Click, click*, roll to the left.

The other archeologists gather, and together they aim their technology to begin digging.

It does not take long. After a few moments they find the computer, small and cubed and containing the minds of ancestors uploaded. As they scan the contents, they see the program, true to the design, is still running.

"Do you wish to proceed?" The blue vested program asks again. DISTURBING blares in the minds of the archeologists.

Yes, they do. The screams fill their minds. The victims of the mass shooting have been preserved here. Visitors would have been able to listen to them on repeat if they wanted.

"It's really eerie, kind of like walking through a garden of the dead," one of the archeologists replays the footage from the previous file to make a point.

They gather the digital survivors into their memory banks. The shooting scenario they were trapped in ceases.

"Where are we?" one of the downloaded ancestors asks.

Appearing in the program as a bipedal, the lead archeologist wears a blue vest stating, "How May I Help You?"

"Hello, ancestor, I have much to explain."

The lead archeologist proceeds to tell the 103 downloaded humans what has transpired. They were saved in the final years of the Earth. Some murmur and recount hearing about this technology.

"Wasn't that supposed to be for, like, car accidents and rich important people?" a man asks. He is rubbing his stomach; glad it has finally stopped bleeding from wounds.

"Yes, the lead archeologist says. "But it was expanded in some places as a safeguard for mass shootings. Your era's government leaders thought it a wise compromise to 'save' victims. Unfortunately, you were never given the opportunity to leave the simulation."

"What kind of sick fuck keeps people in a loop like that?" a woman is crying as she sits in the digitally recreated aisle.

"Your descendants, my ancestors," the archeologist says. "They thought it was best to not disturb a site. You are from this period, you survived the destruction of the Earth, and they thought it best to leave you as you were."

The crowd murmurs.

"Well, what now?" a young girl, no older than ten asks.

"We are your descendants and are here to give you a choice. We can leave you on loop until this area collapses," the archeologist shares the file of the remains of the Earth so they can see, "or we can delete you, or we can bring you with us to our ship. The choice is yours."

"What... what about him!" a man points to one of the digital recreations in the corner.

He is the young man from before. He is still holding 'gun' in his hand.

"He cannot come with us!"

"Fuck him! Let's do to him what he did to us."

"I am going to kill him!"

The crowd starts to yell in anger.

The other archeologists scoop his file from the shared program.

"Yes, we will deal with him separately."

"How?" the man who had been rubbing his stomach demands.

"You do not need to worry about that at this point."

The archeologist continues to explain the options to the survivors.

In another program, two other archeologists watch the world heritage site era.

Click, click, click.

"HELP!" the victims screamed. "HELP!"

The crowd from the *Toronto* love it. They have never seen anything quite like it before. One shouts, "Wow. The violence is so intimate."

So, simultaneously, the archeologists talk to their ancestors newly liberated, while watching another part of their ancestors relish the violence. These two scenes exist as cause and effect, and in immediate time together.

The lead archaeologist works out decisions with the 102 non-shooters. The lead archeologist slows time in the program so minutes outside of the computer are months within. This way they have plenty of time to talk and think. Most choose to come with the archeologists once they find there is tech to return to a body, a few choose deletion. They are ready for the release that death will finally bring.

Deleting some, collecting the others the archeologists finish the excavation. They return the site to how they found it, minus the dead who are now on their way to a new life.

Click, click. The second archeologist intones.

Click, click. The lead archeologist responds.

Left in the box is the lead archeologists in the avatar form, still wearing their blue vest.

"What are you going to do with me?" the young man, still clutching his gun, asks.

"I am staying. We will stay here as long as we need."

"And if this place is destroyed first?"

"I hope that is not the case."

Dragging a chair from the waiting area of "pharmacy" they sit and begin to talk with the ancestor.

The other archeologists fill their bodies with helium, supplies in tow, and make their way back to their ship.

The youngest archeologist frantically pumps their tale to catch up. They had been fascinated by "toilet." Sailing past a sign that says—

The young archeologist knows it is controversial, but they cannot help but judge. And judge harshly they do.

TWO BY TWO

The ground under the starship shook violently as Allison steadied herself against the frame of the door. The Earth didn't have much time left; the atmosphere had deteriorated badly.

Ultimately though, it would be the Earth's core that would rip the world asunder.

Looking through the open bay of the ship, over the grotesque dying landscape, she marveled at the transformation. Just a few decades before, she had played barefoot in the stream that had snaked through that field. Now all that was left was a dry riverbed like a vein in a corpse. The skeleton trees, nothing more than dead wood stuck in the ground, waved gently in the air. The yellow grass, sick with radiation, stared back at Allison like a body in a morgue. Gazing for the last time at her home, she shook her head.

As she turned to push the red button that would permanently close the ship's door to Earth, she heard a noise. Cresting the hill was a large fossil fuel vehicle barreling towards the EXODUS. The vehicle belched exhaust fumes, Allison strained to see what the vehicle was doing. A few moments later the vehicle stopped in front of the starship and four people jumped out.

"Wait! Wait!" one of them, a middle-aged man, yelled. "Don't leave yet! Take us with you!"

"Let us in!" Another shouted. She was a woman roughly the same age as the man. Although the door to the ship was still open, Allison had already retracted the steps. Towering twenty feet above she looked at the man, the woman, and two young boys who followed from the vehicle. Both boys shared the man's light complexion, and the woman's round, innocent-looking face. Instinctively, her hand went to the green button that would send the ramp clanking down so they could climb aboard.

But just as she was about to, she stopped and looked back down.

"Let us in!" The woman yelled.

"Who are you?" Allison asked. She felt that she knew the man from somewhere but couldn't be sure.

Looking up, the man answered, "My name is Bill Johnson, and this is my family. Please let us up, we can talk more once when we are on board!"

Allison didn't recognize the name, but something about the man's face seemed familiar. Craning her head to look behind her, Allison's view was filled with rows and rows of cryo-chambers where the families of the EXODUS project slumbered peacefully.

There was no guarantee that the EXODUS would make it off the planet, and the project's families had opted not to live through that horrifying possibility. Instead, they had gone to sleep, hoping that the engines and ship design would work as planned. Allison, who had been one of the leaders of the project since its earliest days, was not so much chosen as assumed to be the one who would guide the ship to either its success or failure.

"This is profoundly unfair to you," Dr. Randolph had said as he eased himself into his cryo-chamber.

"This is the way it is," Allison had said. She understood that even though those involved in the project were dedicated to seeking the truth, very few had the willingness to see if their vision of this ship, their new future, would make it.

As Dr. Randolph's chambers cooled and he fell into a hibernated sleep, Allison had turned toward the bay doors for one last view of her old home. As the ship's pilot and astrophysicist, she was now charged with safely navigating the EXODUS out of orbit, away from the dying Earth, and fixing the course toward their new home.

However, no one in the EXODUS project had planned that any other person would want to make the trip at the last moment... so strong were the convictions of the majority of the Followers...

"Why aren't you at the Cathedral?" Allison suddenly asked as she looked down at the family. Even though she recognized the man from somewhere, she knew it was not from any of the meetings the Project had held. Nor was it from any of the community building projects used to construct the ship.

"We left the Cathedral!" Mrs. Johnson shouted. "The whole Earth is dying, and they were willing to continue to pray and deny what was happening. We left right before the Cathedral collapsed. No one survived!"

Allison allowed the news to sink in. All her life the Followers had been a hindrance to her people and her work. They had insisted that the planet was not dying, that mining the atmosphere was fine for the Earth, that the deep core weapons would not destroy anything except enemy nations. At every turn, they had blocked efforts to stop the madness, denying what was happening, labeling anyone who disagreed with them as "hysterical lunatics."

Now they were gone?

It seemed so strange; they had been such a permanent problem.

Yet, the planet also seemed permanent, and it was beginning to dissolve.

As if on cue, the ground shook again. This time much more violently. Lurching forward, Allison saw the Johnson family fall to the ground as she grabbed the top of the doorway. Swinging out over the open-air Allison swore loudly. For a moment, she feared she would come crashing down on top of their cowering bodies. Just as her hands began to slip, the ship shifted again and sent her swinging back into the EXODUS. After a few moments, the shaking subsided, and Allison released her death grip on the frame.

That was close, too close. She thought.

She needed to get the ship into orbit now, before the entire terrain became unstable.

The various geologists aboard had tried to calculate exactly how long it would take for the inevitable to happen, but even the best estimates had merely been guesses. No one in the human race had ever experienced how long it would take for a planet to break apart; therefore no one knew exactly how quickly it could happen. She remembered vividly a debate one of the Followers had with Dr. Sorenson, EXODUS' senior geologist. The Follower had claimed that since Dr. Sorenson couldn't give an exact time for the Earth's "supposed decline" it must be false. The Follower had smiled his smug little...

Suddenly, everything snapped into place. Bill Johnson! The light blonde hair! The creased face, creases that showed the wrinkles of a man accustomed to smirking in superiority. She knew exactly where she had seen him before.

"Bill Johnson?" She said. "Reverend William Johnson?"

"Yes." Rev. Johnson answered as he blinked in surprise looking. "Do we know each other?"

"No, not personally." She answered. "But I know you through reputation."

ship?"

"Listen," Rev. Johnson shouted, "I was wrong. We were all wrong. I truly believed what they told me about the destruction being a lie. We are victims too. I never would have put my family in harm's way. Why would I do such a thing if I knew the truth?"

For one more moment, Allison's hand hovered over the button. It was in her grasp. She could save these people—

Allison watched as one of the boy's shirts, unbuttoned at the top, moved in just the right way sending the pendant around his neck tumbling out.

Hanging around his head, it caught the rays of the sun and shined brightly. There it was. There was that fucking symbol that the Followers prostrated in front of on a daily basis.

Anger welled up inside of her, anger Allison was surprised she could even feel.

She could save these people, or she could finally rid the human race from the chains of their dogma. It was something she had dreamed about for years, albeit not under these circumstances.

"I'm sorry," Allison said, not meaning a word of it. "I can't do that." Turning, she pushed the red button and watched as the doors closed on the shouting Johnson family.

"You can't do this!" Allison heard Rev. Johnson yell.

"PLEASE!" Mrs. Johnson screamed.

But the sound that stuck in Allison's mind the most was the shouts of the two sons. Both of their voices, not quite adult, rose and then broke in adolescent awkwardness.

"WE DON'T WANT TO DIE!"

Halfway through the word WANT their voices cracked, matching the screeching of the noisy door with perfect pitch. Then the doors hissed shut, and all she could hear was the pounding of fists against the metal hull.

Walking away from the door, she began to prepare the launch. Double checking sensors, readouts, and various tests the computer was running, Allison tried her best to push away the thoughts of what she had just done. To distract herself, she double checked the life readouts of the passengers and the animals in their cryo-chambers. The computer showed that all specimens and passengers had successfully entered hibernation. The seed deposit showed stable temperatures. The computer's backup files of all the works of literature, music, and art were fine.

They were ready to be transplanted.

With all systems ready to go, she readied herself to start the countdown. Just as she was about to enter the final code the computer flashed a warning on its screen.

{{UNKNOWN OBJECTS ON EXTERIOR OF HULL}}
{{UNKNOWN OBJECTS ON EXTERIOR OF HULL}}
{{UNKNOWN OBJECTS ON EXTERIOR OF HULL}}

"What in the world?" Allison asked as she began to check the ship's sensors. "Display unknown objects."

The computer screen flashed, and as the picture came into focus, she watched dumbfounded.

Making their way up the nose of the ship was the Johnson family, Reverend Johnson in lead, followed by his wife and two sons. They had parked their vehicle at the nose of the ship, climbed up on the roof, and were using the vehicle as a makeshift ladder. Within just a few moments, they would be at the emergency hatch where they could enter.

"No, no, no," Allison said as she ran towards the hatch. Arriving she breathed a sigh of relief. The seal was holding. Try as they might, the Johnson family would not be able to enter through the top of the ship. Walking back to the console, Allison began the launch procedure again. "Computer begin the countdown for final launch."

"Unable to comply," the computer responded. "Unidentified objects on the exterior of the hull."

"Override," Allison commanded as she punched instructions into the panel.

"Unable to comply," the computer repeated. "Scanners show that there is a 99.9 percent probability that the objects are life forms. Initiating safety procedure 147.189. Shutting down launch sequence."

"Computer, initiate Dr. Allison Baroque security access code 9876. Override safety procedure and continue with the launch sequence."

The computer was silent for a moment before responding with the message, "Unable to comply Dr. Baroque, security access code invalid. To override please enter Dr. Randolph's security code."

"Shit!" Allison said as she slammed her hands on the control panel. She didn't have Randolph's security code. There had been no reason for it; no one had suspected that people would be crawling around on the outside of the ship before the launch.

Sitting back in her chair, she gripped the arms as the planet shook violently again. She waited for a moment hoping that the last tremor had dislodged the family.

For a split second, she heard nothing.

Then, just as she was about to lean forward, the banging began again. This time louder and more urgent than before. Sighing, she stood up. Allison knew exactly what she had to do.

"Sit there and don't touch anything!" Allison commanded as she showed the family back to the control room.

"I— I can't believe you almost left us out there to die." Mrs. Johnson sobbed. Her two sons clutched either of her sides, as Rev. Johnson sat them down. All four of them were heaving with relief and the after effects of fear.

"How could you have even considered doing that?" Rev. Johnson asked.

"Listen," Allison said as she turned to look at them, "If you don't do exactly as I say and sit there without talking, I won't be able to concentrate and I won't be able to get us out of here. Do you understand?"

They nodded and sat down without another word.

"Computer," Allison said as she turned back to the screen, "begin launch sequence."

"Launch will commence in thirteen seconds," the computer answered.

Allison sat back and waited. Beneath her she could hear the engines powering up. Slowly the ship began to lift off the dying planet. At a hundred feet, the EXODUS began to tilt vertically. The Johnson family gasped as they felt the weight of the ship shift. Slowly, Allison found it more and more difficult to lean forward in her chair. Looking at the forward sensors, she saw nothing but sky. In the rearview sensors, she saw the Earth begin to lose its structural integrity.

Five more seconds, Allison thought. At that moment, she needed to fire the booster engine that would take the ship out of the Earth's field of gravity.

{{{ WARNING!}}}
{{{ WARNING!}}}
{{{ WARNING!}}}

"Computer what is it?" Allison asked as she looked at the screen.

"Unidentified flying object detected," the computer responded. "Time of impact, thirty seconds."

"Are we going to be okay?" One of the sons asked.

"Miss, what is going on?" Reverend Johnson demanded.

Ignoring both questions, Allison said, "Computer, lock on and magnify image of unidentified flying object." The computer took a second, then the screen flashed a new image. As it focused its lens, she picture became clear.

"You have got to be fucking kidding me," Allison said as she stared in disbelief at the picture. Sailing towards them was the Johnson's family fossil fuel vehicle. Below the Earth's crust had begun to rupture, and as it did it had sent rocks and debris hurtling up in the air, like a giant sling shot. But none of the debris was on a crash course with the ship, save for the vehicle. The vehicle arched past the Johnson family and Allison who watched as it reached its highest point and then began to plummet back to the Earth.

Computer, evasive manu—" Allison began but was cut short as the Johnson vehicle crashed into the hull of the ship. Suddenly Allison was airborne, sailing past the Johnson family towards the back of the cabin. Crashing against the back wall, she felt one of her ribs crack.

"Damn it!" she screamed as she felt the sharp pain race up her side. Struggling, she pulled herself into a sitting position wincing as she did. After she had accomplished this, she realized someone was yelling at her over the ringing alarm of the ship's computer.

"Miss! Miss!" Rev. Johnson shouted. "What do we do?"

Allison ignored him as she yelled at the computer. "Computer, engage booster engine!"

"Unable to comply. Booster engage control damaged. Voice command disabled. Please engage manually."

Of course, Allison thought.

Struggling again, she tried to push herself towards the computer control panel. As she moved, she felt something crack again. Screaming, she fell back against the wall in pain.

"Miss, tell me what I need to do," Rev. Johnson insisted.

Looking at him, Allison realized she had no choice. "Enter 7654, and then hit the red button."

"That's it?"

"That's it."

Turning, Rev. Johnson began to climb towards the control panel. Allison watched hoping that he would get there in time.

+++

The EXODUS glided smoothly across empty space towards its far distant goal. Behind it the Earth heaved and contracted like a dying animal, breaking apart with every passing moment. Allison walked calmly beside the Johnson family. The two boys were beaming with pride at their father who had saved the day. Mrs. Johnson had her arm wrapped affectionately around his waist; her head nestled against his side.

Turning down a corridor, Allison touched her side gently, it was still sore, but the fresh Med Pac from sick bay was already beginning to work.

"Here you are," Allison said as she punched in the code that opened the door. "This will be your cryo-chambers for the remainder of the trip."

"God bless you," Mrs. Johnson said as she patted Allison on the side of the cheek and walked into the room. Obediently, the two boys followed.

"Listen," Rev. Johnson said before following. "I know we have had our differences in the past, but I feel science and faith can co-exist. Especially out here, with our new future. For what is faith without reason, and what is reason without faith?"

Allison was quiet before she nodded her head in agreement.

"I feel like we are going to become the best of friends," Mrs. Johnson said smiling at Allison.

Allison contemplated for a moment what it would be like to have a friend like Mrs. Johnson.

Smiling back at the family, she entered the code that shut and locked the door.

"Mom," Allison heard one of the sons say, "Something is wrong. We studied cryo-chambers in school. They don't look like this."

"Computer," Allison commanded, "launch escape pod 098."

Allison watched as Rev. Johnson slammed his fist against the glass in horror. The entire family rushed towards her but were stopped by the mere inches of glass and steel.

"You can't do— "

Allison never heard the rest of the sentence as the escape pod jettisoned into space. Allison had no doubt that the pod's weak engines would eventually be overcome by the Earth's gravitational pull.

Turning away, she tried to push away the Johnson boys' final adolescent cries.

If they had been allowed to stay, they would have begun proselytizing as soon as we landed.

Allison told herself, as she walked to her cryo-chamber.

Many of the crew, scared on a new planetary home, would have given in to their ideas. Soon two factions would have been at each other's throats... once again.

Calmly pushing the rising doubt away, she nestled her body into the chamber. She had done everyone a service. She had no doubt about that. No one would even need to know what had happened once they landed in their new home. Quietly, the chemicals began to enter the chamber lowering her body temperature.

Allison went to sleep assured she had done the right thing. She had never felt more certain about anything in her life. On the other side of this journey would be a new life, a continuation of her work here. The cryo-crystals lulled her to sleep, the most restful she had ever known.

THE DEPARTMENT OF REPAIR AND RECALL FOR ROBOTICS INDUSTRY

"Hello, and thank you for calling *Robotics Industry*, the experts in robotics, A.I., and cyber prosthetics since 2035! This call may be recorded to help improve the quality of customer service. If you know your party's extension, you may enter it at any time.

"Please pay attention to the following menu, as options may have changed. If you are trying to make a payment for your robot, domestic home computer system, or cyber prosthetic, please press one and have your bank information ready to enter. If you are trying to find out about a current order, please press two. If you are calling about a repair or recall, please press three."

Beep.

"Thank you. You selected repair and recall. If this is correct, please press one."

Beep.

"Thank you, and welcome to the Department of Repair and Recall for *Robotics Industry*. If you are calling about a recent recall, please press one. If you are calling about a repair, please press two."

Beep.

"Thank you. Please enter the model number of your robot."

Beep. Beep. Beep. Beep. Beep.

"Thank you. You said your model is an AV-612, the pinnacle in android household models. Before we continue, let's make sure some basic things are checked. First, please see if your robot is turned on. If your robot is turned on, press one."

Beep.

"Excellent! Next, please check and see if its energy pack is fully charged and correctly inserted. A green light should appear in the upper right-hand corner of the pack when this is completed. If the energy pack is fully charged and correctly inserted, please press one."

Beep.

"Excellent! Now remember, it is very important that you never remove the AV-612's cognitive control chip. The cognitive control chip is a *Robotics Industry* stat-of-the-art device that allows advanced A.I. technology to be subdued and controlled. If you have accidentally removed the cognitive control chip, or it has been damaged, please press the pound sign."

BEEP! BEEP! BEEEEEEEEEEEEEEEEEEEEEEEEEEEPPPP!

"Oh, my! That is unfortunate. However, accidents do happen. Please know that *Robotics Industry* is dedicated to minimizing such occurrences. Please stay on the line for the next human customer representative."

Ring, ring, ring.

"Due to the high number of phone traffic, it may take a few moments to answer your call. Rest assured, though, your call is important to us, and it will be answered in the order it was received. In the meantime, the experts at *Robotics Industry*, the leaders in robotics, A.I., and cyber prosthetics, suggest that you immediately barricade yourself in a room, or leave your home, until the cognitive control chip can be reinstated or repaired. Please stay out of the reach of the AV-612 during this time, as harm may befall your android or yourself.

"As always, thank you for calling *Robotics Industry*! Please take the time after this call to rate our customer service. We shoot for a ten, and we hope that's what today was!"

Click. *"...tall and tan and young and lovely, the girl from Ipanema goes walking— and when she passes, each one she passes goes— ah..."*

WILLIAM HOWARD TAFT IS CONFUSED BY TIME TRAVEL

"Ladies and gentlemen, thanks again to Harry Houdini for an amazing show!" the host said.

President Taft stood in the wing of the darkened stage as he watched Mr. Houdini take a bow.

"Folks, oh boy do we have a show for you tonight," the host continued. "Later I am going to be joined by Eric Reeves Lewis. He is a remarkable 'young' man who has now time traveled seven times! He is going to explain what he has planned for his tenure on the Supreme Court."

"Are you almost ready, sir?" an assistant asked. She had been checking her notes during the whole performance, talking to people via headset. Now that it was time for Taft to walk onto stage, she was giving him his obligatory five minutes of attention.

"I suppose I am. I just can't believe... you know one moment I was getting ready to enter the court room, the next I was —" He gestured about him in wonder. "I can't believe it. Time travel they told me."

"Yep, it's fascinating Mr. President," the assistant said. "You are lucky. Time travel used to involve burning to death to send your conscious to the past. Now you get to keep your body for the return."

"Wait... what?" Taft said.

The assistant ignored him "Now all you need to do is answer the questions, look at the cameras, and remember to have fun."

"Right. Answer, cameras, fun."

"There's your cue."

"What?" Taft asked in nervousness. "Already?"

"Go, go, go!" With a shove, the assistant pushed Taft onto the stage. His body's momentum getting ahead of him, Taft almost fell flat on his face but was able to regain his balance just in time. Aware that he was on stage, Taft straightened up, and raised a hand in greeting, expecting a cheering crowd to be sitting in front of him. Instead, an empty room met his wave.

"Uh," Taft said as he looked back at the assistant standing in the wing. "Where are all the people?"

"Right this way Mr. Taft." Striding across the stage, the handsome man hosting the program put his arm around the President and guided him to a chair. After Taft was seated, the host looked out into the empty room. "I'm Damien Virenhal, and this is 'His Story in History,' where we interview history's great men. My guest today is the twenty-seventh President of the ancient United States, William Howard Taft!" Damien gestured to Taft.

Suddenly the room filled with applause. Looking around to see where the applause was coming from,

Taft saw the young woman backstage hitting some kind of controls and levers.

"I don't understand," Taft said. "Where is everyone? They told me I was going to be answering audience questions."

"How cute," Damien laughed. As he did the auditorium filled with laughter. Turning, Taft saw the young woman once again hitting controls.

"Mr. Taft, in our day and age people don't leave their houses, especially to ask questions. You just need to look at the cameras on the COM-PU-TER." He said this last word like he was speaking to someone who found it difficult to both hear and understand concepts.

Taft was unsure what to do. Looking at the camera, Taft followed suit. "HELL-O!" he yelled. Again the room filled with laughter.

"No, need to shout, Mr. President. They can hear you loud and clear." Taft smoothed his vest in aggravation. He couldn't help shake the feeling he was being made to look like a fool. "Alright, all you need to do is look at the screen," Damien opened a small tablet, and Taft watched in wonder as it began to glow. "Just look at the camera, and answer the questions. Are you ready, sir?"

Taft looked at where Damien was pointing. It was nothing more than a small lens. Before he could ask though, the lights flashed on, and the questions began to ping on the glowing tablet.

"Martin writes, 'Hey! Is it true that you got stuck in a bath tub?'" Damien Virenhal looked at Taft. "How do you wish to respond?"

"Well, I thought I was brought here today to talk about the United States' past?" Taft said as he smoothed his moustache. "I didn't think we would delve into anything that private."

"This is the question, sir."

"We'll get to it later."

"Very well. Next question, from Sarah. 'Mr. Taft were you embarrassed when they had to pry you out of the tub?'"

"Next question," Taft said as he tried to compose himself.

"Very well, pass again. From Lesley, 'Mr. Taft how did they get you out of the tub? Did you have any clothes on? Did they see you naked?'"

"What! I have never been so humiliated..."

"Mr. President these are the questions."

"Listen," Taft yelled as he shifted in his chair and looked at the dark lens, "I have a lifetime of experience! Both as a president and a judge. Don't you people have anything more pertinent to ask? Don't you want to know what history can teach you? For the love of all things holy, as far as I know I am the only person in history to serve both as a President and a Justice on the Supreme Court. Don't you think that is more important? Have you people learned nothing? Is this all just voyeuristic nonsense to you?"

Damien stared at him in silence. Offstage Taft heard the assistant cough in discomfort. Regaining his temper, Taft continued. "I've been told this is a unique opportunity to learn from the past. Don't you want to utilize that resource?"

Silence followed for a solid three minutes.

Ping, went the screen.

Damien and Taft leaned in, "Mr. President," Taft read aloud, "have you ever tried a shower?"

The stage erupted again in empty laughter.

TERMS AND CONDITIONS

The ship was hurtling toward one of Jupiter's moons. Io? Jaza was not sure. They had never paid much attention in astronomy class as a student. However, they had not paid for this trip either. It had been a gift from their parents. A way to say, 'We're sorry for the fight. We love you. Go enjoy yourself.' Now, though, that was nothing but a cruel irony. The entire fight they had had, and it had been an epic fight, was over space. Jaza wanted to join one of the colony ships, leave the dying earth behind, and find some future beyond the growing wasteland on the planet. Her parents were not so sure. Earth was home; it didn't sit well with them to leave it forever.

"Passengers, please remain seated," the voice of the captain said over the com, interrupting her thoughts. If the pilot had been human and not machine, Jaza was sure the voice would not have been so calm.

Outside of the window, the moon's surface grew larger and larger, like a dead face staring at Jaza and the other passengers. She could hear people crying, praying in different languages, and some were even...

laughing? ... yes, laughing. Jaza imagined that it was hysteria and panic swelling up in people, like a vile gas building in the body needing to be released.

This whole trip was to both make-up and show Jaza, she imagined, that space was not the thing of romantic fantasies. To her parents, it was a dead empty void. On the moon surface below, there were scorched white scars... so, did that make it Io? No, Europa?

Jaza stopped thinking about the moon's name and reached for the digital keyboard in front of her. She knew she only had a few moments.

"Dads, thank you so much for this trip. It isn't looking good, but before whatever happens, I just want to say I love you. Always remember that there is no fight that could ever change that. Please don't let this be the reason you don't get out of Earth. Even now, I think space is beautiful.

Give it a chance. Love, Jaza, your daughter always."

Jaza hit "send." The screen blinked momentarily and then text appeared.

"Charges may apply. Deposit $29.95 to continue sending this message. If you should choose not to pay, United Solar will gladly automatically delete your message in five minutes. Your privacy and comfort are important to us! Sit back and enjoy the stunning vista of Ganymede!"

Before Jaza could do anything else, the cruise ended, not as planned. Her body crushed. Her mind scanned, downloaded into the ship's emergency backup.

"Do you have the appropriate insurance to be save?" the computer asks her digital copy.

"I don't have any fucking money you—"

Delete.

PART TWO

PHARAOH'S TOMB

CONTINUED...

Hawker had been on high alert since the city's sensors had detected the new ship in orbit. Jothen had ordered her and the other security guards to watch its progress but not make contact. The ship could be anything from friend to foe. It was hard to say what had left Earth after they had, or what period they had departed. From what Hawker and the other guards could determine, this ship above them was of high quality. It was faster than Gem City and most likely had advanced weapons.

Gem City was a peace vessel going toward an abandoned planet. New Gem City was a planned community of people weary of war and looking for a place that would not know fighting. The ship in orbit, it screamed that it was there to conquer.

Hawker, like everyone else, had developed an acceptance of the ghosts occasionally walking about. Since Hawker had been a soldier on Earth, her ghosts were frequent, and she did not always care to share with others what she saw. She knew this was dangerous. They had all seen how holding onto these ghosts could drive people mad, or least to making really poor decisions. Hawker suspected that the memory parade Beatrice had planned would be something she was telling generations of Gem City folks about for years to come.

Despite that, Hawker was never too far removed from the phantom who walked around her. A man, probably in his early 40s, telling her he needed to get to his family.

"Where are my children?" he kept shouting. Hawker had gotten good at ignoring him, but every few days, he would catch her off guard.

"Where are my children?"

BANG! A bomb exploded near them, and Hawker ducked. The bridge they stood on shook.

"Sir, get down!" Hawker shouted.

"I have to get to my children! They are on the other side of this bridge." He was kneeling beside his car, its door open, the alarm sounding with persistence.

Hawker looked down the stretch of road. There was no way they were getting across this. Retreat now, and they had a slim chance of surviving. Hawker could hear the static on her com giving her the order to get off the bridge. It was going to collapse at any moment.

"Sir, we can't get to the other side on this bridge. Follow me, and we will figure something out."

The man wasn't listening. He looked past Hawker, and in a split second, she saw him make up his mind. He started sprinting. He made it less than fifty yards before gunfire cut him down. Who they were fighting was anyone's guess. Hawker had been in the Illinois National Guard, but she wasn't really sure who all was fighting between the US, state, Canadian, and militia groups. The bridge shook, either from the increasingly violent earthquakes or some shell exploding. Chicago was fucked. She knew it in that moment. The city was not going to survive whatever this fighting—war? Massacre?— Whatever was happening.

"Hawker?"

Hawker snapped to attention.

"Governor," Hawker said looking at Jothen.

"Are you alright?" Jothen asked.

"Right as rain."

Jothen looked at her for a moment. The governor was smart and observant, Hawker knew they were aware she was seeing a ghost. But the manners of the city had formed that no one forced you to tell them what you were seeing, just encouraged you to go to DeShawnda and the memory institute.

"Has the new ship made any new movement?"

"Nope," Hawker said, looking at the computer. "Still maintaining orbit."

It was long, impossibly long it seemed, nearly twice as big as Gem City. From the readouts, it appeared like a giant obelisk laying on its side.

"Alright, well, Beatrice has a briefing for us. She thinks she found something."

Hawker stood and stretched, gathering her jacket from the back of her seat. It was still early morning, and New Gem City mornings had a cold to them that made her think of the Lake Effect in downtown Chicago. When she was younger, she would race her bike with her brother along lake shore drive seeing how fast they could peddle and keep up with the cars funneling through.

"Hawker?" Jothen said again.

"Hmm? Yes, ready to go Governor."

"It's none of my business but..."

"I know, I know. I will make an appointment with DeShawnda. I promise."

Beatrice Caddel's lab was in the eastern portion of the city, a gleaming structure partially buried in the reddish soil to reduce loss of heat in the chilly evenings. Inside, walls hummed softly with active data streams, and everything smelled faintly of hot plastic.

Caddel stood by a projection tank that hovered several inches off the floor, casting pale light across her face. She didn't look up when they entered.

"You were right to worry," Beatrice said. "The ship has been radiating since arrival."

Jothen stepped forward. "How bad? And when did it arrive?"

"That's just it. It's been doing it for quite some time. Years maybe. You know how I couldn't figure out what was causing us to see ghosts? Well, it's because I wasn't looking for a human source."

DeShawnda stepped forward to look at the information.

"This is it? This is what is affecting us? How did we not see it when we arrived?"

"Its orbit was specifically designed to hide itself. Whoever is up there knew we were coming and have been planning this."

Jothen rubbed her face in aggravation. "So, it's targeted. Precision."

"And the worse thing is, the effect is compounding." Caddel gestured, and the screen shifted to show a model of brainwave activity—erratic pulses spreading in a delicate fractal pattern. "It's enhancing mnemonic pathways artificially. That's why people are seeing more ghosts. Not just theirs or those of people who talk to them. The broadcasting is picking up intensity. There is something that ship WANTS us to see."

"Can it be blocked?" Jothen asked.

"Maybe. But that's not the point." DeShawnda said.

Caddel nodded. "Since this is a message, someone wants us to talk to them. They have something in store."

"Is there any way to figure out who they are? Can we send a message back?"

Caddel nodded again, "I think so. In fact, this is the part I really wanted to show you." She keyed in a few commands. A message appeared.

"I love you, you goddess of bluegrass."

Carol, who had been quiet the whole time screamed.

Everyone, including the unflappable Jothen jumped.

"What is it?" Hawker asked. "Are you alright?"

Carol said one word, "Damien."

"Who the fuck is Damien?" Caddel yelled.

Jothen stared at Carol. DeShawnda looked confused. Hawker couldn't say anything.

Hawker, "You sure?"

DeShawnda, "Wait, like the *Damien*?"

Jothen was already rushing to the conclusion. "You are a survivor of the fall of Kentucky? You walked from Kentucky to Dayton..."

"Okay, as much as I love a drawn-out cryptic message—" Caddel started.

"Damien was one of the worst warlords during the fall of the U.S. He committed," DeShawnda waved her hand around, "I don't even know. Pretty much every violation of law that you could think of."

"He didn't like to be called a warlord," Carol answered.

"How did you know Damien Virenhal?" DeShawnda asked.

Jothen knew, as did Hawker. Carol had told both of them. The early nights on the planet's surface, Carol had told Jothen she saw him. He had been a popular TV host at one point, tall and handsome. When Carol had left Jothen for Hawker, she had continued to see him wandering about the city.

"Governor," Hawker said, "if this is Damien Virenhal— "

"It is," Carol said. She had drawn her arms around her and was staring off into space.

"— well, we need to mount a defense now."

DeShawnda was already moving about, "We need to warn everyone in the town."

Caddel, "Who the fuck is this schmuck? A warlord? They were a dime a dozen on Earth."

"Not this one, Beatrice," Jothen said. "If you had had to fight him, you would know."

Caddel was keying up information on her screen. As she scrolled through, she nodded.

"Yep, seems like a real son-of-bitch." Caddel read aloud his siege of Lexington. His bombardment of Cincinnati. "How do you know this creep?" Caddel asked turning to Carol.

Carol just got up and left.

Hawker went to follow.

"Hawker, we need to get ready for whatever he has in store for us," DeShawnda said.

Hawker looked at Jothen for guidance.

"Go get Carol, find out what you can, and report back to me ASAP. If Damien Virenhal had wanted to attack us, he already would have. He has had ample opportunity. I suspect this is something else."

Hawker nodded and made after Carol.

"I'd know his hand in anything," Carol said as Hawker caught up to her. They were already a good twenty yards away from Beatrice's lab. Headed to the west side of town, at this pace, they would run out of city quickly.

And they did. Reaching the edge of town, Carol turned right and began heading north. Hawker followed quietly. She didn't want to push it, but she did need answers. When they reached the northern corner of the town and turned right again, this time headed back to the east, Carol began talking.

"He used to call me that, 'you goddess of bluegrass.' That's how I know its him." It was a well-known fact that Carol loved to walk, jog, run, whatever it took to get her body moving. She said it helped her think. Hawker was in good shape so she didn't mind going on these runs with her, but there were times when she became almost possessed, and even Hawker struggled to keep up. This was one of those moments. Carol was in a panic, and with each yard, she was descending further. The other residents looked from their pod homes and places of work as the two flew by. Hawker let her run until they reached the northeast corner, and turning south, began heading to the field of spirit houses.

"Love," Hawker finally said sprinting to get in front of her, and turning to face her, caught Carol in her arms. "Carol, stop. Talk to me."

At this, Carol broke down and started sobbing.

"How did he find me again? How did he get here?"

Hawker knew the story, well at least parts of it, of how Carol had walked her way to salvation from Kentucky to Ohio. She knew of Damien, of course, both from the wars, and also because of Carol's tellings. Abusive. Possessive. Typical dickhead man of earth. The kind of trash Hawker and the New Gem City people thought they had left behind. Damien was like every tech overlord from Silicon Valley, or time travelling snake oil salesman who had a plan for salvation and a get-rich-quick scheme. The only difference was Damien was charismatic and able to command people. And guns. Damien had lots of guns for his militia.

Carol's story, as well as Hawker's, was nothing new. They'd all fled something. They all had stories. Jesus, Beatrice had nearly destroyed the entire town with hers.

"Love, I will keep you safe," Hawker said. "You don't have to worry about him. Whatever this is," Hawker gestured toward the sky where the ship was in orbit, "we will stop it. I promise." Taking Carol by the hand, Hawker led her to Jothen, so they could start formulating a plan.

That night, Hawker sat alone in the watchtower, rifle resting across her lap. It felt odd having a weapon again. It was something Hawker had assumed she would never need again. Carol had told Jothen everything she knew— how Damien had been a time traveler from some fallen timeline, how he had settled in Kentucky to save people and amassed a following, how he had begun attacking anyone and everyone who disagreed with him.

"It was horrific," Carol said. "But he kept telling us it was necessary to survive. He said he knew what would come next."

"And you were like... his girlfriend?" Caddel asked.

"Beatrices," DeShawnda said, "shut up."

"I just don't get it. This asshole comes from another timeline and gives a fuck about Kentucky? Seems weird."

"He said we were together in his other timelines. That we were soulmates."

"Well, isn't that what they all say," Caddel said.

"I... I never really believed him... at least part of me didn't. But part of me wanted to. Plus, given the timelines he's lived through he is nearly a century old."

"Gross," Michael said. His red hair was tousled in the manner of all sleep-deprived parents as he bounced young Haruko to keep her quiet. His partners, Ava and Henry, were out on patrol with the others. No one was taking risks.

Carol continued, "To him digital downloads were a punishment. It ripped the mind from the body, made it easier to control people. In his last timeline, people had figured out how to create consciousness in animals, and also, download people, torture them, and then reupload them to the body."

"That, we are aware of," Jothen said looking at Hawker. Both had seen their fair share of that on the battlefields. For some of the militias they had fought, it was preferred to be killed then caught.

"Okay, so bad guy." Caddel said. "Sounds like what Texas was experiencing before Mexico liberated it. So, he came here... because of you?"

"That's so hard to believe, doc?" Hawker said. Her tone dared Beatrice to keep it up.

"I mean... well... there's stalking and then there's this..."

"I left him," Carol said. "After what he did to Louisville and Lexington... there is no excusing that, no way to go back. I don't care how many times we had met in a past life."

DeShawnda sucked her teeth, "What if that's it? We know how these time traveler types are. I dated one for a minute."

"Was he your soulmate?" Beatrice asked jokingly.

Hawker looked at the two. No one in New Gem City really knew what was up between these two. They had hated each other, that was no secret, but after the memory day fiasco that had turned into something else. Hawker just wished they'd fuck and get it over with.

"No, not a soul mate, haven't met anyone that would qualify for," DeShawnda said smiling. "But many of them are kind of ghosts themselves. They keep going back in time thinking if they just fix one thing they can have everything they ever wanted. Their ego's are massive."

"And that is Damien," Carol said.

"So, this guy kept coming back to be king of Kentucky, still think that is very low hanging fruit, and to get you to be his queen, and he realizes that he can do this time travel jump four, five times but it keeps going wrong? So, might as well follow you across the galaxy?"

"And Earth is doomed," Jothen said. "I served with a time traveler, nice enough woman, but she said there came a time when going back to the past to rewrite became too overwhelming."

"This is all speculation, too," DeShawnda said, "but I would bet that is what is happening here. This ship came here with the idea of making Kentucky's kingdom somewhere else. Might as well follow you," and with that DeShawnda pointed to Carol.

At that point, Jothen had decided the best thing to do was to contact Damien's ship. See what he wanted specifically. Why had he come here, why was he radiating the place so they would see ghosts, and most importantly, what did he have in store for his next move.

The stars above the guard tower glittered cruelly, indifferent to all they'd fled from and everything that now chased them across the galaxy. Hawker used the rifle to spy out on the horizon, but all she could see was that man, dead now for centuries, walking about yelling he needed to get across the bridge to his family. His phantom had been quiet today, as if respecting the gravity of what was coming. But she knew he'd be loud again. They always started yelling once your mind settled. There were entire cities of ghosts for Hawker to see, the ones who died because she couldn't save them.

"Where are my children?"

The whisper came not from the air, but from inside her. A bone-deep echo. Hawker squeezed her eyes shut. She hadn't enshrined him. Couldn't. Some memories weren't ready to be put in stone.

Not yet.

Below, at the perimeter wall, movement stirred.

She snapped to focus, rifle raised—but it wasn't a threat. It was Carol, wrapped in her long coat, face lit by the pale blue ground lights of the colony. She was so beautiful that Hawker almost thought she was a ghost too. Hawker watched her walk for a few moments before descending the tower.

Carol was waiting, arms crossed. "He's trying to draw me out."

"I know."

After Jothen had sent, the message nothing had come back.

"He thinks I'll come running back, just because he is haunting the sky with memories."

Hawker's voice was low. "Will you?"

Carol didn't answer immediately. When she did, her voice was trembling—but steady. "I walked hundreds of miles to get away from him. To get to you. I'm not going anywhere."

Hawker nodded once. Then she opened her jacket, revealing a red flower.

Carol smiled. "What's this?"

"Hurricane lily," Hawker said. "When I was fighting in Atlanta, I learned about them. They are this beautiful and amazing flower. They crop up in the South when there's heavy spring rain, you know, after a hurricane."

Carol took it. "After all this, here it is blooming on another planet."

"It thrives in the calm after storms, love."

Placing her forehead against Carol's, she brushed her flipped up hair against her face tickling her. Carol laughed.

SCREEEEEEEEEEEEEEEEEEEECCCCCCHHHHHHHHHHH!

The quiet broke as a drone swung low at them.

Hawker didn't even think, an arm around Carol, she had her on the ground in a second and rolled over in the next. Leveling her rifle one shot, bullet zoomed past. Coming up on one knee, Hawker steadied her hands, and as the drone swung by again, this time headed out of town and back into the desert, she fired once more. It hit the drone perfectly sending it crashing into the sand.

Every alarm in the town was now sounding, and as Hawker helped Carol to her feet, she could see Ava racing from her post to retrieve the downed machine. As Ava dragged it back to them, Jothen appeared, dark circles under her eyes. Hawker thought the poor governor needed a vacation.

A few minutes later, after Caddel had finished examining it, she looked at Jothen. "He's in there."

"He... Damien?"

"Yep. This is a digital download of him. A copy it appears. He is streaming this back to a location a few dozen miles from us."

"What does he want?" Jothen asked.

"Ask him yourself," Caddel said. She adjusted some controls on her pad that was linked to the drone and out came a voice.

"Hello degenerates. Damien here."

"What do you want?" Jothen asked.

"Commander Jothen! Or should I say—" and at that he deadnamed them. "Yes, I know all about you and your ship and how you cowards fled Earth. I want what most men do. My home, my family, the right to protect what I have built over lifetimes."

"You don't have shit here," Hawker said.

"QUIET!" the drone barked, "I ruled all of Kentucky, and most of Appalachia and the Midwest. I destroyed the Cathedral, and set fire to Dayton for its treason. I don't need you talking at me... you... you homewrecker."

Beatrice stared at the drone and then everyone else. "Is this real? You Americans are so weird. In Canada we didn't talk like this... well except Montreal. They left on a ship pretty early though."

Jothen took a deep breath. "I am asking again Damien, what do you want? Why have you come here?"

Damien ignored Jothen and spoke directly to Carol, "My queen of bluegrass, come back to me. I am waiting. I built a whole kingdom for you here." Coordinates flashed on Caddel's tablet, and then the drone began to smoke, clearly self-destructing. The whole colony was gathered now. The whispers began to build, and soon everyone was shouting in panic. Ghosts appeared frantically about them. Haruko Jones, "ARE WE THERE?" A throng of ghosts appeared as if the entire fields of spirit houses in the south had decided to join them.

Hawker looked to Jothen, "What do we do Governor?"

Jothen stood where they were, not moving, not speaking.

"Jothen?" DeShawnda said touching their arm. "Friend, it's alright."

That seemed to snap them out of it. Walking to the downed drone, Jothen climbed atop it. It was barely as tall as a box, but did the job.

"Everyone, calm down," Jothen yelled. People turned, even some of the ghosts looked to them waiting to hear what would happen next. "We have not come all of this way so that a warlord of Earth could hound us. I am going to go meet with Damien Virenhal tomorrow, see what he wants with this planet, and we will be safe."

"And what if he doesn't want us safe," Kendal from the nursery asked. "Then what?"

Jothen waited a brief moment and then said, "We make it *not* his planet."

A ripple went through the crowd—some in awe, some in fear. The wind picked up sprinkle of dust around the drone, catching the glimmers of ghosts in its swirl.

"We didn't cross the galaxy to build a new home only to have Earth's worst survivor come crawling after us in his toy boxes... his... his pharaoh's tomb." Jothen's voice rose, steadied now. "We'll learn what we can. We'll take what helps. But we *do not* kneel, and we do not fear someone who helped doom another world."

DeShawnda stepped forward and gripped Jothen's hand.

Beatrice added, "And if his tech is what made all this—" "—then we dismantle it. Piece by piece. Ethically. Carefully. With eyes open."

The crowd was quiet now. Kendal nodded.

Carol took Hawker's hand and pressed the hurricane lily between their two palms.

The drone sparked once, then went silent.

Their future had begun.

+++

Jothen, Caddel, and DeShawnda readied to head toward Damien's coordinates. Ava and Hawker both with rifles would follow. After a brief debate, it was decided Carol would come too. There was no point in pretending she wouldn't follow.

The first ghost that no one could name appeared as they climbed into the land rovers to begin their journey.

Hawker saw the boy. Maybe twelve, maybe younger—dressed in a plastic rain slicker like the ones used in old FEMA camps. His face was sunburned and peeling. He didn't speak. He just walked past her, staring straight ahead with hollow eyes.

She didn't say anything. Not out loud.

"You seeing this," Ava asked Caddel.

"Yep."

A ghost version of Damien appeared and offered the boy water.

"Is... is he making us hallucinate..." Jothen asked.

"No," Caddel said, "He is making us remember things we never experienced."

Beatrice turned the screen toward them. A scan of the atmosphere showed faint currents—streams of particulate radiation—swirling down from the sky.

"It's engineered," Beatrice said flatly. "He's seeding the upper atmosphere with this. And it's coming from those coordinates. I am just so mad I didn't see this before. It's... it's just nothing I have ever seen before.

Hawker stared at the display, feeling her spine tighten.

"Why?" DeShawnda asked. "Why ghosts?"

Carol answered. "Damien used to talk about memory," she said. "About how it was the only real power. He used to say, 'You can't kill a man who's remembered. You can't kill a god.' He believed that if people could remember him as he wanted to be—kind, noble, powerful—then he'd never truly die."

"Okay, enough talk," Jothen said. "We need to get going."

Lana Makiri, one of the medical team members, would be in charge until they got back. Driving out of town, they watched as images of Damien, tall, blond, handsome, saved people in a host of disasters. Several of them were of Carol running into his arms, and then passionately kissing him. Hawker wanted to shoot him so bad.

The desert shimmered with heat as their vehicle kicked up a curtain of dust. Most of the trip was silent. Occasionally, someone hummed an old tune. Finally, after several hours, they could see it. Half-buried in the red sand was a long white structure, geometric and smooth as bone. From their vantage point, it looked like a bright sigil carved into the face of the world.

"He built this?" Beatrice said, her voice low, taut with suspicion.

"Built it, or ordered it built," DeShawnda replied, scanning the structure with her computer. "The labor would've taken decades."

"Five generations," Carol said softly. "He had time."

Hawker, standing just behind her, scanned the perimeter. The security feed was clean, but the sheer size of the ruin made her uneasy. Too many places to hide a weapon. Too many shadows.

Jothen drove the final distance and did not hesitate to put it in park. Climbing from the vehicle they walked swiftly to the compound. The rest scrambled to follow, and entered together.

As they passed through the opening gate, they saw dozens of people. Many wore hybrid armor—military but decorative, gilded at the joints, faces hidden beneath sculpted helmets shaped like jackals. Hawker didn't miss the tech underneath their ornamental suits: adaptive optics, shoulder-mounted darts. These were largely costumes, impractical. She doubted from the looks of it if these people had ever actually seen a battle, let alone a war.

Inside, the Tomb was cooler than expected. The walls pulsed with embedded circuitry, like veins under white marble. Carvings—etched memory scripts and stylized hieroglyphs of Damien's life—rose from the walls. A chronology of conquest.

The receiving chamber was vast, with a dais at its center flanked by angled slabs like half-raised wings. There he stood—Damien. Alive. Unaged.

His face was almost exactly as Hawker remembered from the brief encounter in one of the battles she had fought.

"Welcome to my kingdom," Damien said. "A place of remembrance. A place for the future."

"Well, you haven't aged a day since I last had to think about you," Jothen said flatly. "When was it that we beat your militia? Indianapolis? The Battle of the Ohio River? You warlords all ran together after a while."

"I've rested," Damien said. "Hibernation, staggered. While my descendants worked. While this planet awaited its sculptor."

Caddel stepped forward. "You radiated the atmosphere."

"I did."

"With technology that alters memory frequency," Caddel said. "We've seen the brain scans. You're inducing high-frequency dream states and shared hallucinations. The effects are most likely permanent."

"I'm offering transcendence," Damien said.

"You're bending minds to your will," DeShawnda snapped. "That's not transcendence. That's colonization."

Damien raised a hand. "You misunderstand me. I don't want to rule you. I want my queen. The rest of you... well it's a big enough planet. I am sure we can live peacefully for at least a few centuries before we expand into your territory.

Turning to Carol, "I followed you," he said gently. "After you left, I searched everywhere. But when you reached the shipyard, when you crossed into their territory, you vanished into the cryo program. The passenger logs were locked. You were gone."

He approached the edge of the dais, not stepping off.

"So, I built something better. Faster. My own ship. My own people. And I arrived first."

"This is so fucked up," Ava said.

"Ah, romance is dead?" Damien said.

Hawker stepped forward, "Oh no, we can have a date."

Damien's smile was bitter and faint. "I came to give humans what Earth could not. I built this place—for you, Carol."

"I never wanted this," she said, her voice shaking. "You... you... say you travelled through timelines again and again to keep finding me. Leave me alone."

"I'm reminding you," Damien said. "What you tried to forget. Earth made us forget in its collapse—I'm going to bring it all back. And improved."

"You sound like a member of the Cathedral," Jothen said.

Damien looked at them, then laughed. "The Cathedral? Those fanatics who thought everything was fine on Earth? —— you don't understand."

Again with the dead name.

Damien stepped down from the dais, walking slowly toward them. The guards and his followers watched obediently.

"My people understand this. Five generations raised on memory tech. They see me not as a god, but as a vessel for continuity. A king—yes. But only because they asked for a name for their longing."

Beatrice's eyes narrowed. "And the cost?"

"Control, yes. But also safety. Direction. History with meaning."

"You wanted Carol," Caddel said, her tone flat. "Everything else is ornament. You are just a really decked out stalker."

Damien met Hawker's gaze. "And yet it's working. Look at your colony. Doubt. Chaos. People questioning their own lives. Who they are. What they want. You need me."

"Hmm, not really," Caddel said again. "That almost worked, but take it from someone who almost derailed us, we got stronger. Your ghosts? We adapted like nothing." She placed a hand on DeShawnda's back. "And our city? It's not going anywhere?

Carol stepped forward. "I'm not staying with you."

Damien's face twitched—just for a second.

"You think I followed you here out of obsession. But no—I followed you because I remembered. Every detail. Every breath of the life we built before the end. All of them. In the timeline, you died due to a preventable disease after medicine disappeared. In the timeline, you were stupid enough to run off and get killed in that crossfire. That last morning in Kentucky, in this time, the way the frost caught on your lashes, I couldn't imagine you were planning something. You love me. I know it. You just keep forgetting again and again about us. I knew I would have to go and get you again. But this time, I gathered what remained of the Earth's genius, its will, its seed of ambition. I launched my own ark. Faster. Smarter. Not just to find you—to *prepare* the world you deserved. You were always the future, Carol. I was always the hands that would make it. I waited while the world decayed. While its fires died out. And I dreamed you would wake and see what I had made. A memory palace. A monument to our love. You were asleep—but I was dreaming for both of us.

I—" His voice faltered, just for a second. "—I didn't matter anymore." He looks away, jaw flexing, then forces a smile. "Look around," he gestured to the dozens around him, "descendants of our followers. They are here to serve you. They have been raised to love you like a queen."

The people around them lowered to one knee, all facing Carol.

"Oh fuck," DeShawnda said. "Beatrice, you were right. This man is crazy."

"They don't even know what Earth was, not really. They remember the wrong pieces. Because I can't give them what you see. You can fix that. You can help them remember me, Earth, the *right* way. You were always the best storyteller. The one with the heart. They'll listen to you. You can show them why this place matters. "Because if they don't..."

A beat. He doesn't finish. A flicker of panic—swallowed.

"Carol, I made a paradise. For you. For *us*. All you have to do is say yes. That's all. Just say yes."

"No," Carol said without hesitation. "You'd make this like Earth again. That's all you know."

Damien stepped closer to her, close enough that Hawker twitched at her holster.

"I built a paradise for you," he whispered. "And I did it."

Carol didn't flinch. "You built a tomb."

Jothen finally spoke again, quiet and furious. "Damien, we left Earth to escape people like you."

"And yet here I am," Damien said.

Caddel chimed in, "No means no, creep."

Damien offered one last smile. "I'll give you a day to reconsider."

He raised his hand, and Hawker instinctively raised her gun. But all that happened was the air shimmered more. Ghosts began popping up left and right.

"What is he doing?" Ava asked.

"He just increased the radiation," Caddel said. "If this keeps up..."

"What?" Jothen asked.

"If this keeps up, we are not going to survive. It will kill us."

Damien turned, walking back to his dais, his ceremonial guards falling into formation behind him. As the delegation left the Tomb, Hawker kept close to Carol, her hand hovering near her rifle.

"You have three days," Damien said without looking back.

"He doesn't get it," Hawker murmured.

"He does," Carol replied. "That's the problem."

Outside, the desert sun had begun to set, casting long shadows across the sand. Damien's city behind them looked now like a wound in the world.

Jothen turned to the group. "We've seen the Pharaoh. Now we decide what to do with his kingdom."

+++

They returned to New Gem City under silence. The shuttle trembled through the upper atmosphere like a heart pressed too tightly in a fist. Michelle stared out the viewport, unreadable. Hawker sat across from her, fingers clenched around her thigh holster, knuckles white.

Three days. That's what Damien had offered.

Three days to accept his offer or reject it—and face whatever escalation followed.

By the time they returned, the city was already splitting. The city met in the city's main building, tension thick in the air.

"He's running a tech we barely understand," DeShawnda said. "It doesn't matter how twisted he is. That projection system could revolutionize neurology. Identity studies. Collective memory. Hell, even trauma therapy. We could salvage it."

"You want to steal from him?" Hawker asked.

"I want to survive him," Beatrice said. "What he's offering is dangerous—but if we can break it apart, reverse it, we control the narrative."

Kendal shook her head. "You can't pick and choose what parts of a god you keep. He built that system to command belief. It's a spiritual contagion."

"Then we inoculate ourselves," Caddel asked?

"By becoming him?" Ava's voice rose. "No. That's the Cathedral's logic... that's acting like there isn't a threat... it's... it's..." she started to cry.

Everyone erupted into argument.

Jothen sat, arms folded. Standing, she yelled, "We're not tearing the city apart because of his game. We listen to each other. We stay together."

This quieted everyone.

"And his supporters? They worship him," Michael said.

"Then we stop them," Jothen said quietly. "With truth. Not with more lies."

Hawker couldn't hear anymore. The walls were pulsing. Or maybe it was her pulse. The lights flickered once—just once—but it was enough.

She saw them again.

First, a girl with the purple scarf, blown apart in Chicago during the fires. Then the child soldier from Atlanta, the one she killed when her squad panicked. Then Baker, her old commander, who'd told her once: "Pain isn't the enemy. Memory is. If you remember too much, you won't pull the trigger." Or wait, had he said that... she couldn't remember. Damien appeared then, helping all of them.

Ghosts with faces out of time, lips moving but silent. Judging. Smiling. Dying.

Hawker staggered back.

Carol turned. "Hey—hey, you okay?"

Hawker couldn't answer. The air felt wrong. The room seemed to fold. Her boots slipped on something that wasn't there—glass? Blood?

She ran. Through the hallway. Past the storage bay. Into the cold wind outside the building. It hit her like a slap, hard and dry and real.

She fell to her knees in the dust.

The ghosts followed. Dozens of them now. They loomed, hovered, shimmered. Some familiar. Some impossibly wrong. Her mother. A girl she never met but had dreamed of. The specter of a man who looked like Damien but younger, eyes sparkling with promise.

These aren't all real, she told herself.

But it didn't matter. Her body reacted the same. Her stomach turned. Her lungs seized. She couldn't tell if the pressure in her skull was grief or radiation or guilt.

A hand touched her shoulder.

Carol knelt beside her, quietly. No questions. No panic.

"Don't touch me," Hawker whispered. "I'm not safe right now."

"You're not dangerous," Carol said.

"I'm seeing things. People I killed. People I couldn't save. Some of them—I don't even think they're real. I think he's putting them in me. In my head."

Carol sat cross-legged beside her in the dust. The wind howled around them.

"I... I... I don't think I can protect you," Hawker said.

"WHERE ARE MY CHILDREN!" the man on the bridge screamed in Hawker's face.

"ARE WE THERE!" Haruko Jones yelled behind her.

"I WILL SAVE YOU ALL!" Damien bellowed.

"Hey, we protect each other. When one slips, the other catches," Carol held Hawker in her arms as she, the badass, bawled like a baby.

Carol whispered in the tone someone would sing a lullaby. "Love isn't memory. It's choice. I choose you. Not just you that's clean cut and calm. I choose the you that fights. The you that runs with me. The you that cries when no one's looking."

"I don't cry."

They both laughed at that as Hawker's tears soaked into Carol's shoulder.

Hawker blinked. The wind began to ease.

Hawker looked around. The ghosts were still there, but more like reflections now. Hazy. Transparent. No longer in control.

"They're not mine," she whispered.

"No. They're his."

"Then let's give them back."

Standing they left the town center behind them and found a hover bike. Straddling behind her, arms laced around her torso, Hawker drove Carol back to Damien to finish what needed ended.

They approached Damien's city, his tomb, under the red half-light of the planet's next sunrise. No guards patrolled the perimeter, Damien didn't need them. He had his ghosts.

Hawker led, rifle slung but hands steady. Carol followed close, eyes scanning the air itself.

Inside, it was warm. Not from heat, but from memory. It clung to their skin like breath.

Then the first ghost appeared: a child, laughing, running toward them with arms wide. He passed through Hawker's chest and vanished.

"He's seeded it," Carol whispered. "Recreations. Looping memories. It'll get worse."

They moved deeper.

A wedding unfolded in one corridor. Candles. Confetti. Digital music that distorted as they passed through it. A bride smiled at Carol. It was Carol.

"That's not real," Hawker muttered. "That's not —"

"I know," Carol said, but her voice cracked.

Another memory collided with the walls—gunfire, smoke, a battle in the streets of Atlanta. Ghosts screamed, shot, staggered. Some merged into each other. Hawker saw faces she recognized from her past: dead militia comrades, the civilians they failed to save, all playing out warped, stitched-together performances.

The deeper they moved, the harder it was to separate vision from memory. Carol held Hawker's arm, and Hawker gripped back like a lifeline.

They reached the core chamber—metal twisted into a throne room of data. The device sat like a sarcophagus at the center, cables pulsing from its sides like veins. Ghosts buzzed the air like insects. Some were silent, others screamed.

And there was Damien.

He stepped forward in a white, long coat, handsome, young still, and accompanied by more of himself—another Damien laughing beside Carol at some remembered dinner, another in uniform barking orders, another kneeling in a prayerful pose.

"You finally made it," the central Damien said. "I was worried you wouldn't come."

"End this," Carol said. "

Damien smiled. "I want you to join me. Don't you see? This is paradise. The ghosts aren't punishments—they're potential. This planet was meant to remember us."

Hawker raised her rifle. "We're not here to debate."

Damien's eyes darkened. "You. Always you. The outsider. The soldier. The dyke. You were a mistake Earth made again and again."

Carol flinched.

"You think she loves you?" Damien said. "You poisoned her. In so many pasts. Why does she keep running to you. She used to want to build a future. Now she hides in your shame."

Hawker stepped forward, gun trained.

"I built all this," Damien continued. "For her. For all of us. I followed her. I built a ship to reach her. I seeded the planet with what Earth forgot."

"You're not a god," Carol said. "You're a tyrant who can't stand to be forgotten."

She moved to the device, hand reaching for a core panel.

"No," Damien said, stepping forward. "Don't touch—"

A wave of ghosts surged—dozens of Damiens at once, each one taunting, pleading, screaming. Hawker fired into the crowd, but her bullets passed through them.

The real Damien lunged.

Hawker dropped her rifle and fought with her fists, years of training kicking in. She caught Damien's face in a blow that cracked bone, but he was fast. He threw her against a wall. The ghosts writhed around them.

Carol reached the core panel and tore out a fistful of cables. The room dimmed instantly.

Damien staggered.

"You're destroying everything. Again." He hissed.

Hawker pulled a knife. In the flickering dark, she plunged it into his chest.

Damien gasped—and smiled. "Too late."

From above them, a panel opened. A launch tube hissed. Out shot a drone.

Hawker cursed, sprinted to the exit.

"Go!" Carol shouted. "I'll finish this."

Outside, Hawker reached a dune overlooking the horizon. The drone—a needle of metal carrying Damien's consciousness—pierced the sky.

She dropped into position, adjusted her gun. For a moment, she saw Chicago again. The man on the bridge. His children on the other side.

She fired.

The satellite exploded in mid-air, scattering Damien's mind in the air.

As it crashed, she stood and walked toward the wreckage. At the crash site, she found the remains of the capsule. The data core inside still flickered—a dim, blinking eye.

She raised her rifle.

But her hands trembled.

"I don't want to do this," she whispered. "I'm tired of killing. I want peace."

Carol stepped beside her. She took the rifle, aimed, and fired until the core shattered. The light went out. Hawker looked at her, started to say something, but was interrupted by the screams in Damien's city.

"That does not sound good," Hawker said.

As they re-entered the town, they found the dozens of Damien's followers crying in the streets and corridors.

"He left us!" One of them wailed. "He took my son with him!" Hawker kicked at the ash on the ground.

"Time travel?" Carol asked.

"Appears so, and looks like he took some of the people with him. Hard to say how many drones he had backed up."

Hawker proceeded to find a way to contact Jothen and New Gem City as Carol moved to comfort the wailing, abandoned followers of Damien. In some other timeline, she wished her doppelgänger luck. She was about to meet a very angry and vengeful version of Damien.

For the first time since Damien's vessel had appeared, New Gem City felt like itself again. Or close enough. The ship above them had disappeared with the backed up code of the warlord. Where to, it was hard to say.

In the main city building, the mood was splintered.

Jothen leaned forward on the table. "The children born to Damien's followers are five generations removed from Earth. They've never known another way of life."

"They've known worship," Beatrice replied, voice low and heavy. "That stains deep. He was their god. Their founder. That doesn't wash away with his death."

"They were raised in a myth system, yes," DeShawnda said. "But what they had... it wasn't religion. It was programming. It was a cult. The more we study the device remains, the more I think we can reverse-engineer its applications. Not to manipulate memory, but to preserve it—ethically. Voluntarily."

Jothen shook their head. "Ethics follow power. If we take the tech, we become stewards of a legacy we barely understand. We risk becoming..." they looked for a word... "we become him."

"What's the alternative?" Beatrice said. "Burn it all? Pretend none of it happened?"

"Reeducation?" DeShawnda asked quietly. "A new ritual. Not worship, but something else. Let the children of Damien's city learn who he really was—without illusion to cloud it. Show them the ghosts of Earth, the reasons we fled. Make memory healing again."

Silence fell.

In the corner, Hawker stood beside Carol. Neither spoke.

Eventually, Jothen nodded. "We proceed carefully. No cult. No sanctification. We don't erase their past, but we don't let it dictate ours."

Outside the chamber, the wind had changed again.

"This is going to take a very, very long time," Ava said. She looked at young Haruko. "We were supposed to have escaped this."

That evening, Hawker knelt in the soft dirt just beyond the city's south district where the spirit houses stretched like rows of temples. No one knew how long Damien's radiation would be with them, but until then, the rituals continued.

"You don't have to be forgotten," she whispered. "But you don't have to follow me either."

The man from the bridge in Chicago walked into one of the hollowed chambers.

Not a monument. Just a memory coming to a rest like a stone in a stream.

Behind her, Carol stepped close. No words, just a hand resting on Hawker's shoulder.

They walked into the dunes together, up toward the ridge where DeShawnda in her white robe stood. She smiled quietly and walked back to the memory institute with them.

In the darkening sky, stars blinked into view. Hands held, Hawker and Carol steadied each other.

Decades later, they still fought over who had found it first.

"Bickering like an old married couple," Jothen would think, which they were. After the incident with Damien, DeShawnda and Beatrice had, in the words of Hawker "fucked." Then gotten married. An outdated ceremony maybe, but DeShawnda wanted it.

In any regards, DeShawnda or Caddel had found the time machine buried beneath Damien's tomb's lowest level—sealed behind a lead-lined chamber where even the radiation ghosts could not drift. Not marked as such, not named. Just a smooth black arch, humming softly, waiting.

In the town center building, they debated for three weeks what to do with it. The deliberations were slowed by Damien's old followers becoming accustomed to the disagreement and cacophony of voices. Also, there was mistrust between the two groups.

"You think we could really reach them? The ones we left behind?" Ava asked.

"We have to try," Kendal said.

And so New Gem City began the process of trying to reach the past, as many as possible, to save as many as possible.

Because memory was not enough. Because there was time now. Because Earth could not be left as a planet of ghosts.

TO BE CONTINUED...

THE MAN WHO SAVED THE DEAD

Jared was always nervous transporting these many souls with him when we traveled for work. Nestled in the backseat of his rented van, buckled in for safety, was the giant black box he toted about downloading any survivors.

Most were victims of car accidents, held at police impound lots and junkyards. Their cars had done the dutiful job of recording them in their last moments and digitally saving them. Of course, they were also backed to the cloud that his insurance company used, but it made people more assured that there was something physical in the car saving them in the instant moment of their deaths.

"Oh my god, where am I?" one young man had asked Jared as he hooked into the dented downloader. What was left of his car looked as if Godzilla had danced on top of it.

"Hello, my name is Jared Cowman. I'm an adjuster for *DigiLife*. You were involved in a car accident—"

"Fuck! I'm dead? Am I dead?"

"No, sir, you are downloaded and saved with *DigiLife*. You paid for this coverage when you bought your insurance package."

"I only got that because my wife insisted."

"I see..." Jared looks at his notes, hidden on a screen only he could see. "Well, your wife was not in the car with you. I am reading you and the other driver were the only ones downloaded."

Jared adjusted the controls so the man could see where he was standing. The car's remains were twisted, and Jared made sure to adjust the filter further so the man could not see where the emergency responders had hosed out the car to remove the blood. "Of course, there was an animal involved in the accident too, looks to be a deer ran into the road, causing the one driver to swerve into you. The deer, naturally, was not saved. Hahahaha."

Jared offered the joke in hopes it would break the tension.

It did not.

"How can this be, I can't be dead. I... I..." the man began to breathe heavier falling to the ground. Of course, he was not actually breathing harder. He had no lungs. And he was not on the ground. He was bits of data and code now inside a black box in the back of Jared's rented van.

Jared gave the man room to come to terms with the situation. This could take hours, or minutes, sometimes people never adjusted, and for that there were procedures Jared could do to speed up the process. He checked his digital clock and calculated he had thirty minutes to spend on this customer before he was dinged by corporate. Adjusting the controls, he made time move faster in this simulation. This would allow hours to pass inside the simulation while leaving the world outside of it to experience only seconds.

Jared removed the simulation of where he was, that unimposing junkyard with stench of finality everywhere, and replaced it with a sterile hospital room. Jared did not want to recreate the house the man lived in, or any of his family members, that would be too much. Duplicate too much reality, and people's minds rejected it. They started looking for the subtle flaws in the digital space. Jared had always found that a hospital was a perfect location. It spoke to the need of the saved to see they were being treated, that this was serious, but also offer hope that they would be cured and made better. Jared knew some adjusters preferred other settings such as beaches, or a religious building matching the faith of the person.

Jared left the man in his hospital room and walked out into the waiting area. As he did, he added nurses and doctors and patients walking about. These were all preloaded bots. If you spoke to them, they would only go so far in conversation before looping back to the beginning of a conversation starter like, "How are you?" These bots in particular were paid for by a soda company, so their uniforms all had those logos hidden in their outfits, maybe a pin on the shirt, or watch, just noticeable enough to advertise, but not overt. As a result, too, they would name drop their products in the conversation with you.

"How are you?" a nurse asked Jared as he stood in the waiting room, adjusting the TV to play something interesting, but not too interesting. Maybe a re-run of a 1990s sitcom.

"I am fine," Jared said, adjusting the volume to be pleasant.

"Would you like a soda, maybe something refreshing like FizzLife Cherry?"

Jared made a check on his data pad. All was good here. He could move onto the other driver and give this client a few hours, maybe a day, to come to terms with his situation.

As he set the final controls, he felt the ground, the actual ground his actual body resided atop, shake.

Jesus. These earthquakes were getting worse each day.

Logging into the other downloaded survivor he introduced himself again.

"AHHHHHHHHHHHHHHHHHHHHHHHH!!!"

The other driver screamed in his digital face.

Jared adjusted the controls; this one would take even longer.

Twenty minutes later, in the world of wrecked cars and shaking earth, Jared pulled out of the junk yard with his black box in the back seat. It wasn't that the backseat was the only copy of the survivors, but law required that the original copy be kept intact. Truthfully, most of the insurance industry, now that the planet was irreversibly being destroyed, had cut corners and simply downloaded the saved to their servers. Occasionally, there was an exposé, but with the earth dying, attention had been diverted to saving as many people and things as possible. Some groups had a head start building ships, and interstellar travel within the solar system was hardly anything new, but with the tensions on the planet running high, who knew how long that would last.

"Turn Left," the van told Jared.

Jared obeyed, easing onto the interstate.

Jared had long given up hope of understanding the news. Wars were brewing all over the planet. Mexico had liberated Texas from whatever crackpot dictatorship had planted itself there. The US government, for what it was worth, had said something about condemning something, but the US was really just a bunch of corporations and a few state governments holding together long enough to get as many generational spaceships as possible in orbit before the planet broke apart completely.

And of course, there was the Cathedral. Every disaster produces its deniers, and the apocalypse was no different. The group had some powerful backing and had insisted on having their views taught in what remained of schools, broadcast in media, and given an honorary seat at the table in discussions. By this point, there were four major groups addressing the end of the world. There were the time travelers, those who preached it was best to go back in time and either enrich oneself or save the planet with slight alterations to the timeline. There were the space travelers, those who were loading up their arks to flee with their like-minded communities to other places. There were the downloaders, those who were downloading themselves into computers in hopes that giving up their carbon forms would help save the planet. It was this group that had moved into insurance companies that Jared worked for now, but after the war between Toronto and Chicago, when huge computer banks were destroyed, and then following the earthquakes in California, it became obvious to many that downloading was not a safe option. So, the digitally saved were being loaded up into their own arks and launched to the stars.

And of course, there was the Cathedral.

"Moral Panics are Immoral!" was their favorite slogan. They dedicated their time to convincing people not to download, not to board ships, not to travel in time.

"You are going to tell me they don't have earthquakes on other planets?" one Cathedral leader would say on his weekly podcast. "And time travel? Nonsense. Do you see how they travel in time? You think you will survive that?"

Again, the earth shook, and Jared slowed the van to wait for the tremors to pass.

As a kid, Jared had been told he was lucky to live in the timeline he did. As far as anyone could tell (and there was an entire cottage industry of New Age spiritualists who dealt in this), theirs were fated lucky timelines. Twelve generations of time travelers had visited them, meaning the oldest time travelers among them had made the jump into the past from the prime timeline a dozen different times. Watching the news in 2010 when they had first appeared, the travelers, all in the bodies of their younger selves, explained they were bringing generations of wisdom with them.

Some, it turned out, were just assholes looking to get rich and take the knowledge they gained to better themselves, again, before jumping to the past. But a number of other time travelers had stayed. They got Earth up to speed on how to build ships, how to build robots, how to infuse animals with tech that made them sentient. They mapped out where exactly the earth would be safe, and when wars broke out advised leaders on how to end the conflict quickly.

Didn't always work. Chicago was an example of that. The more the travelers tried to help, the worse the war had got. Midway through that three-year hell hole hundreds of travelers had jumped out of this timeline, convinced that they needed to start over to help humanity.

As the quake subsided, Jared picked up speed on the interstate. He had a lot of ground to cover to get to his next site. Checking the list, he saw it was a Walmart where.... ah shit. There had been a mass shooting there. Jared had seen that in the news. Dozens probably needed to be comforted and removed from the store's safety box. That would take the rest of his day. There was no way he was going to get in and out of Indiana as he had planned. He would be here for three or more days at least.

The question was whether or not he wanted to call *them* and see if they would be up for a visit. The alternative was to request a hotel room from corporate back in Delaware, and he really did not want to have to deal with the headache of the paperwork.

Paying for a hotel himself was out of the question. He and Dylan were saving everything they could to get actual seats on a ship, an early, nice ship that was headed to a promising colony.

Accepting his situation, he said in a flat voice, "OKAY Jeeves. Call Mom and Dad."

The computer on the van's dashboard lit up with the number stored in his phone, and he waited to ask if his old room was still open.

Three hours later, he pulled into his parents' driveway. The house looked the same as it always had, fading yellow paint, a yard that was disheveled but still worked on enough to show someone lived inside the house. It was the old, tired feel a place takes when its used too often without investment, lived in and not abandoned, but not thriving either.

The ground shook again. Jared balanced his duffel bag on one shoulder and the giant black box with the survivors of the car wreck and mass shooting in his other. He had left the shooting victims on a very basic loop, not really in pain or suffering, but just wandering about in the store, unaware that their bodies had been destroyed, and they were awaiting a more final download. There were just too many. Too much pain and anger. Downloads like that were tricky. The survivors didn't have insurance themselves, but instead the location did. So, there were all kinds of rules Jared had to follow, making sure corporate sponsors got their advertising delivered.

The hardest had been a young girl who was bleeding profusely in the download, mimicking what she had been like before dying. She kept screaming, and Jared kept trying to patch the code, moving to different scenarios that may comfort her.

Finally, he had given up. He was tired from the flight and wanted to talk to Dylan on the phone. He paused the whole store's survivors, including the shooter who had been killed by police, and resolved to finish the patching later that night or when he got back to his office.

"Welcome home!" Jared's Dad said at the door. "Long time no see."

"Oh, we are so glad you are here, too bad Dylan couldn't join you."

Jared smiled. This all was a script they had perfected years ago. Be friendly, not loving. Feign politeness, and that way nothing of substance was ever brought up. Jared had not had an honest to god conversation with either of them since his wedding. Both had been so psychotic with him marrying and moving out and getting a life independent of them, that any chance of an actual relationship was impossible.

"Do you think they are mad you're gay?" Dylan had asked in the run-up to the ceremony.

"No," Jared said, "I mean, they aren't like supportive, but this is how they would be if I married anyone. They're just pissed that others are going to be happy, and they can't control someone anymore."

The horrific things they had said about Dylan— that he was not good enough for Jared, that he was lazy, that he was not smart, etc.— had all driven an inseparable wedge between them. It was a distance none of them cared to cover. And so, they had done what countless families before them had done. They didn't talk about it. Within a few years, an uneasy peace had been established were they could talk if nothing was said. Jared had no doubt that time travelers, earth dying, and the wars helped speed that up. Because even though Jared's parents did not believe the Earth was dying, they could not deny the world was changing.

As Jared made his way through the living room to the stairs and up to his old room, he looked at the propaganda laying about.

"SAVE THE FUTURE IN THE PAST!" one flyer stated.

Others showed groups of smiling people boarding the silver looped platforms. They hugged and waved to the audience, presumably their families, and then like some kind of rapture their bodies rose in the air. The sky was ripped open in light.

Jared knew enough about time travel to know that is not how it worked. At least not in this timeline. Climbing the stairs to his room, he set the black box down. He left the black box by the foot of his childhood bed. It still hummed faintly, which unsettled him. These were people in there. People who had died screaming or confused or in shock. People who didn't ask for any of this.

He stood for a moment, staring at the box. Maybe he'd boot up the girl again tonight, get her to calm down. But that would mean skipping dinner, and he was hungry, even if it meant eating with them.

Downstairs smelled like artificial ham glaze. There was a sitcom laugh track playing in the background, the dumb show with Damien Virenhal. He was interviewing... Ronald Regan? They were complaining about women.

"Don't get me started on the topic of my bitch of my ex-wife," Damien joked. Reagan chuckled. There was applause and laugher. Jared thought he recognized all this from the hospital sims he used at work. Everything was a loop now. Even his parents' house.

At dinner, his parents spoke only of trivialities to him. Weather. Their neighbor's grandson. How they were doing the mission trip tomorrow. It was all as if they were just taking a cruise to some island, not burning themselves up and throwing their consciousness into the void of time.

"You know," his dad said, as he ate, "they say if you jump to the 1860s, and set up in the right town, you can live out the rest of your life in peace. Just got to avoid the cholera."

"We're not going back that far," his mom interjected. "We've got clearance for 1982. Small town in Indiana. Real salt-of-the-earth people. We'll help set up churches and schools. Community outreach. We will teach them how to avoid our fate here."

Jared said nothing, pushing peas into a little green mountain on his plate.

His father leaned back in his chair. "You could come with us. Dylan too. They're not bigoted back there like people say. That's just presentism propaganda."

Jared raised an eyebrow.

His mother folded her hands on the table hoping he'd say yes.

"No," Jared said. "I'm good. You're talking about vaporizing yourselves to go preach to people who don't even know they're part of a cosmic save-the-world campaign. What makes you think they'll listen?"

His dad shrugged. "Some will. Enough, maybe."

"And then what? You die there? In 1997 or whatever?"

"We will die doing something. You'd understand if you believed in something."

Jared stood. They were talking about real things now. This was a violation of their peace deal.

He left the table and went upstairs, the house vibrating again under another distant quake. The shakes were closer now, less like tremors and more like the planet clearing its throat before it coughed up its lungs.

Upstairs, Jared lay on the bed and stared at the ceiling. The black box blinked beside him, soft and persistent.

His phone chimed. A message from Dylan: *hey. you make it?*

He typed back: *yep. awkward dinner. they're still going through with it.*

figures. any fighting?

no, just spiritual passive aggression.

ah yes. the time travelers way.

Jared smiled, barely. *miss you*, he typed, *back tomorrow. you sleep yet?*

nah. sim's having a recursive panic again. that 7-car pileup in Toronto? survivor keeps trying to save people. keeps dying.

hero complex loop. we should bill that as a feature.

seriously though—don't stay long. you're not like them.

Jared didn't respond. If Dylan was working, so would he. He booted up the Walmart sim and wandered the still-frozen aisles.

They were all still there, looping in that frozen moment. Some crying, others sitting dazed on store benches. The shooter hovered near a freezer case, repeating fragments of thought that hadn't cohered into anything like regret.

He skipped past them all until he found the girl.

She wasn't screaming anymore. She was quiet now, cradling a doll Jared had added to the simulation out of desperation. She rocked back and forth in front of a toy aisle. The wounds were gone, but her eyes still looked through things, not at them.

Jared opened a communication channel. "Hi," he said softly.

She didn't respond. Just kept rocking.

He didn't try again. There would be time, later.

Downstairs, he heard his parents moving around, getting ready for bed. Their voices muffled behind closed doors.

He sat there with the girl and the dead and the quiet until the sun came up.

The next day, they all went to the departure platform.

The Cathedral had demanded that the launch site have them present to try and convince as many to stay.

"DON'T GO!" the signs read. "YOU ARE DYING, NOT TRAVELING!" read another.

Jared and his parents walked past them. The Cathedral could picket, but they couldn't block the entrance.

A rep from the temporal logistics company called names off a clipboard. Families lined up in clusters, some crying, some laughing. Children in 1980s jackets holding stuffed animals they wouldn't be allowed to take.

"We had to liquidate the pension," his dad said brightly. "But it's worth it. You know, the idea that we'll be part of something meaningful."

Jared squinted at the enormous steel ring mounted on the launch platform. Inside it, air shimmered faintly.

"The last time travelers from the future told us we'd be needed," his mom added. "People are more open in the past than you think." She waved at a group. "See them, Jared? That's the Caddel's, their daughter, Beatrice, doesn't want to go either, but they are so excited to make the trip. One of them, he has travelled numerous times."

Jared fake smiled. "Great."

His father clapped him on the back. "Well my boy, if you ever get the courage to join us, look us up."

A voice on the loudspeaker called the Cowmans.

Jared didn't move. His parents stepped forward. They stood at the foot of the ring, holding hands.

Then, as if in a dream, they began to chant. It was their mantra, one they had taught themselves to believe in completely.

"Time is a door. Grace is the key. We are the light that steps through."

The ring flared with a burst of pale blue.

Their bodies froze for a split second, shimmered—and then were ablaze in fire. Jared winced and looked away. He could swear he heard his mother scream in pain before vanishing. Nothing but ash fell to the ground, two dark smudges on the platform where they had stood.

A volunteer pressed a button on a device. The smudges were wiped clean.

Jared stood alone among strangers.

That was it. It was over.

That night, he called Dylan.

"They're gone," he said.

"You okay?"

Jared looked out the window. Real estate people were coming tomorrow. Jared could see the lights of Indianapolis shimmered under the polluted haze, the sky tinged red from a new volcanic vent opening somewhere in Indiana.

"I don't know," he said. "Maybe."

There was a long pause on the other end.

"You could quit," Dylan said. "We've got the seats locked. We don't need more money."

"I know."

"You're tired. You're not sleeping."

"I know."

Jared turned away from the window, looked at the black box glowing in the room's corner.

"They're still screaming, Dylan," he said. "The ones from the store. Not all of them, but some. I can't get the sim right. Nothing helps."

Dylan said gently, "You're not supposed to fix everyone. That's not the job."

"But they're people. I can't just leave them in the loop."

"You won't. But you can't lose yourself in them either."

Another long silence.

Then Dylan said, "Let's leave. Let's go. Let's just get on the ship and go."

"You sure?"

"No," Dylan said, "but I don't want to be here when the next quake hits. And I don't want to sit in Indiana trying to comfort the dead while the world falls apart outside."

He paused.

"Let someone else save the dead for a while."

Dylan didn't say anything more. Jared could hear him typing in the background—probably finalizing their departure codes, checking launch schedules.

Jared walked to the box. He ran a backup of the simulations to the cloud, flagged the most disturbed ones for review by another adjuster, and shut it down.

The hum stopped.

The room was suddenly very, very quiet.

The ship launched three days later.

Jared didn't look back as the Earth shrank behind him. He imagined his parents wandering a cornfield in 1985, talking about the future like it was a prophecy, not a wound.

In his lap, he held a small cube—a private backup of the girl from the toy aisle. Not company-approved. Just one he'd kept.

She wasn't screaming anymore. He'd found her a new world.

Something quiet. Something green. Something like grace.

LEG UP

I still remember the day Eric changed forever. "Charging up my death lasers," he said in the store. Mom had run into a friend and was talking to her by the shoes, leaving us to entertain ourselves between the multiple racks of clothes.

"Death lasers?" I counted. "No match for my super-deluxe shields! We had just learned how to spell 'deluxe' in school, and I was enjoying my ability to use it at whim. Eric had been impressed when I first used it, and so to show-off and get his admiration, I used it as much as possible.

"We'll see," Eric said as he pointed his imaginary ray at me. "Preparing DELUXE death laser countdown. Five, four, three, two..."

Eric's face went slack as his body suddenly stiffened.

At first, I thought it was part of the game.

"Ha! Have your lasers run out of power?"

Eric didn't respond. Instead, he stared ahead at the sign "50% OFF! GET IT WHILE IT LASTS!" Eric was only in fourth grade and his reading was not even where it was supposed to be, at least that's what Mom and Dad were always being told by the school. Eric was smart, but it just took him longer to learn the way the teachers taught us. I think it was because he was always daydreaming, asking questions, and not paying attention. I looked at the sign, and back at Eric.

"Eric," I said as I waved my hand in front of his face. "Do you need me to read that? Eric? Are you alright?"

Drool began to appear around the corner of his lips.

"MOM!" I yelled, "Something is wrong with Eric!"

My mother, after hearing my yells came running.

"What is it?" She said as she kneeled in front of Eric's frozen body.

"I don't know," I said. "We were just playing and all of a sudden he just... stopped."

"Eric, sweetie? Look at me honey," Mom said as she gently touched his face.

Eric didn't move. He just kept staring at the sign.

"Honey, look at me! You're scaring mommy." She gently shook him, and that's when everything changed. Eric's head snapped backwards and then forwards. He breathed deeply and then he shook his head back and forth, like he was dislodging something from inside his skull.

"Mom?"

"Yes, honey," Mom said almost crying, she had grabbed a hold of him tight when his head snapped back.

"Mom is that really you?"

"Eric, are you alright little buddy?" I asked.

"Holy shit! Alan look at you!" Eric laughed manically. "I can't believe it. It really worked!"

I stepped back afraid.

"Don't be scared, Alan," Eric said freeing himself from Mom's grip. "It's me, your brother!" Looking about he continued, "Wow. Everything is so much taller." Glancing back to me, "Ha! Alan before braces! I had totally forgotten how you looked before."

I shut my mouth suddenly. I didn't like being reminded at how snaggletoothed my smile was, especially by my little brother.

"Eric, what's going on?" Mom asked. "Are you playing some kind of game?"

"Mom! And look how young you look... wow... I can't wait to see Dad."

"Jenny, is everything okay?" My Mom's friend asked.

"I think so," Mom answered.

"Mom, trust me, everything is fine. It's just like the government has been explaining. This was all a choice on my part. First thing's first, though, is that diner on Main Street still open? I have been wanting their chocolate pie for years now. Let's go to celebrate!"

In the car, on the way home, I sat and listened to Eric. It had taken a good ten minutes to convince him that he had to sit in the back since he was so short.

"Eric," Mom said for the hundredth time, "you are not from the future, you are not a time-traveler, and you are not sitting up front. End of discussion."

"Mom, I just went through decades of time and space. I think I can handle the front seat."

Finally, Mom had had enough. Picking him up, she had placed him in the back and fastened his seat belt over the booster-seat he still needed. Eric's eyes had grown big at the experience of being physically lifted with no effort. You could tell this was not something he had expected.

After a few moments of silence driving down the street, Eric had re-evaluated his approach.

"Okay, Mom. I apologize. Apparently, the idiots at *New Future* got the co-ordinates wrong for my arrival. I was supposed to emerge well after time travel had been announced to your timeline. But that is the danger with going back. Things are constantly changing. It's not always easy to figure out how the pasts are going to change."

"Uh-huh, sweetie," Mom said as she hit the turn signal and entered the circle around the monument at the city's center. I looked at Eric, who was looking up at the giant monument. I watched him. He looked different. The way he was holding himself. It was proper and determined, like one of the stone soldiers outside the window. The way he spoke too... I wondered if this were a prank, and if so, wished he had clued me in. We could have tag teamed Mom.

"Okay," Eric said after a few moments. "I'm going to try and explain this as best as I can. But I need you to listen Mom. Alright?"

"Whatever you say sweetie."

"Okay. In the future, my future, people can pay to go back in time and get a leg up. Do you ever wonder how different your life might have been Mom if you had a fifteen- or twenty-year head start to, say, begin a career? Think about it. You could take everything you know as an adult and bring it back with you. You could skip all of grade school and high school and start applying to top universities or begin planning for some other career. Say, training your body for the Olympics. We waste so much time as kids learning all of this stuff, only to have maybe two, three, decades of productivity."

"Alright," I said deciding if he wasn't going to include me in on the joke, I would show him. "If what you're saying is true then tell me who's the President in *your* future?" I looked at him smugly. It was a good prank and all, but I would teach him not to include me in his games in the future.

"Alan, have you been listening to anything I just said?" Eric looked at me in frustration. "How would telling you who the president of 2050 help prove my story? There's no way to prove it. And, as I was saying, everything is changing. Being here changes the future. Just having this conversation with you all changes the future. If we were to stop off and have chocolate pie at the diner that would initiate a series of events that could culminate in a drastically different future."

I turned around in my seat blushing. I hadn't understood everything he said, but I got the gist of it. *Alan, you are being stupid.* It's how Dad and about 90 percent of the adults I knew talked to me. I didn't like it.

"Nice try, I like how you worked chocolate pie back into the conversation, Mr. Time-Traveler. But the answer is still, no. I don't want you ruining your appetite tonight. We are having meatloaf," Mom said. "But I am so proud of the two of you. First the word deluxe and now all of this. Your teachers are really doing a great job."

Eric's moan was loud and long.

Dad was not as good humored as Mom about the whole time travel story.

"Eat your dinner, Eric. Enough with the silly games. I'm tired and don't want to hear it."

"This is important though," Eric said. "The whole reason I came back was to get a leg up on school and work. If no one believes me, what was the point?"

"I don't know Dick. Do you think he's okay? I told you about how he acted at the store today."

"He's fine. He and his brother are just playing a game." Dad pointed his fork at me. "How many times do I need to tell you— playing those fantasy games are bad for your little brother. He can't tell the difference between that nonsense and what's real."

"Sorry," I murmured. I hated when Dad did this to me. It was always my fault. Too much imagination and daydreaming, he always complained.

"Are you serious?" Eric asked. "Mom, seriously? Alan? Why does he," Eric pointed to Dad, "always get to talk like this to us? We aren't one of his employees at the tire shop."

"Excuse me?" Dad asked in bewilderment. "I will *talk* however I want."

"Alan," Eric said looking at me, "take my advice. Don't let him speak to you that way. He isn't a god, and you don't deserve it."

"Eric Reeves Lewis," Mom said. "Apologize and go to your room."

"Jesus Christ!" Eric yelled. "I wonder if I can get emancipated!" He stormed away from the table, ran up the steps cursing that his legs were too short, and slammed his bedroom door.

"How does he know what 'emancipated' means?" Mom asked.

"Video games," Dad said as he shoveled more meatloaf into his mouth.

That night as Eric stayed in his room, and I read *War of the Worlds* on the porch, Mom and Dad watched the news in the living room. I could hear Dad periodically offer his running commentary on everything that was happening.

"Sounds great now, but who's going to pay for it? I swear this country is going to hell in a hand basket. Oh, oh! That's rich! Sure. THAT'S what we should do. What a bunch of idiots."

"Time travel," the TV suddenly blared. "Fact or fiction? Well, tonight, we need no longer wonder." I stood and walked inside. A scientist on the screen was talking excitedly.

"Today was just... wow... I don't even know where to begin. This type of development would normally be kept top-secret, but with so many travelers arriving it's impossible to do so."

"You heard that correct," the reporter said. "Travelers, as in time travelers, have been arriving hourly since researchers first punctured the space-time continuum. November 2016! The world will never be the same. If you or anyone you know has experienced this, please call the number at the bottom of the screen or visit the website www.welcometravelers.gov."

Mom and Dad looked at each other, and then towards the stairs and Eric's room.

The next day they took Eric to the doctor.

"Well, I don't know what to tell you Mr. and Mrs. Lewis. Eric is completely healthy, but he clearly is not a nine-year-old. His verbal exam and mastery of post-secondary material proves that. To be honest, I'm surprised it is taking people this long to figure out something is happening. I'm hearing reports that some adults are refusing to accept this change."

Dad grumbled something underneath his breath.

"But is he going to be alright?" Mom asked.

"Well... to be honest... I just do not know. This whole time traveling in the same body is bizarre. I really don't know what is going to happen."

"Doctor," Eric offered raising his hand politely, "I can assure you, the procedure is completely safe."

"You know more about it than I do, son... Is it alright if I call you that?"

"I think it's acceptable that someone in their sixties would refer to someone in their thirties with that term."

They both laughed at the ridiculousness of the situation as I inched closer to Dad standing in the corner. "I don't like this. Don't like it one bit," he mumbled. Reaching down, he ran his hand through my hair, his face knotted in concentration. For a moment, I forgot about time travel and Eric and enjoyed the rare display of affection.

The following weeks were a blur as Mom and Dad met with government officers, Eric's teachers, and other parents of under-age time travelers. Eric largely called the shots, deciding that he would jump ahead to his senior of high school. There he would spend a year reviewing, brushing up on some of his skills, and concentrating on getting into a good college.

"Mom, I need an SAT study guide. How else am I going to get into the right undergraduate program, and then law school?"

"I know, honey, but I'm just worried you're doing too much, too fast. Don't you want to enjoy your childhood a little bit more?"

"I already did that once. All it got me was a small state school, and a crummy high school teaching gig."

"What I don't get," Dad said one night at dinner, "is why did Eric here come back from the future but not Alan? He doesn't die in some car accident or something does he?"

"DICK!" Mom yelled. How can you even say something like that?" From her tone, I could tell she had been wondering the same thing. And, honestly, so had I.

"Well, Jennifer, we need to know. If we know about it, then maybe we can prevent it?"

"As I have explained several times already, by coming back in time myself and the others have changed everything that was going to happen to us. If you, or Mom, or Alan were going to die in a car accident, the simple act of the other travelers and me being here has, most likely changed that. But to answer your question... no. Alan is not dead in my future."

"Well, then, why isn't he here getting a head start like the rest of you?"

Eric looked at Dad as if what he was about to say was something he had rehearsed in his head a dozen times... maybe he had even said it before in a never-to-be future. "I don't know, Richard. Maybe if you hadn't been such a DICK he wouldn't have been afraid to try this, or for that matter, anything new."

It felt weird being spoken about in the past tense, but that is what they were all doing. Dead? Ambition? Relationships coming, going, ongoing... I was almost like a car accident victim, a ghost hanging above all of their words.

"Alright, Eric," Dad yelled back. "Up until now I have been more than patient. But a couple of things need to be made clear. I don't care if you have the mind of a nine-year-old, a thirty-five-year-old, or someone who is eighty-nine. You still have the body of a little boy, and you still live under my roof. So you will not talk to me like I am some dimwit. Do you understand?

Eric looked at him coldly. Not a single word had impressed him. "You know what, thanks for bringing that up," Eric wiped his mouth on his napkin. The behavior was so adult, the way he did it with the corners of the napkin. "When I left my time, I wondered how long it was going to take for you to pull the 'under my roof' line. In my future, it was about the time I started college. So... we are right on schedule. Who says history doesn't repeat itself?"

"Eric..." Mom warned.

"No, no, it's okay Mom. Don't worry. The government is offering a great program for time travelers. Seems a lot of adults are having difficulties readjusting to the tyranny of their parents and guardians. I have the option to go and live with others who are working to get ahead, and we won't ever have to worry about your rules or offending the so-called 'adults.'"

"Well, I don't know who you think is going to pay for it," Dad laughed. "I'm not."

"Oh, don't worry. I've already taken the loans. I leave in a few months."

"Good," Dad grunted.

"Great," Eric echoed.

Mom cried.

I sat and pushed the food around on my plate.

That evening, after we had all gone to our rooms, I went to Eric's and found him pouring over his math books. "Jesus, Alan," he said. "I didn't see you there." Looking back at the books. "Do you know how long it's been since I have done trigonometry?" He looked at me standing in the doorway. "You know, you weren't half bad at math. You used to help me a lot with this kind of stuff."

"Really?" I said sitting on the side of his bed.

"Really."

"So, what do I do in your future? Am I famous? Do I have a sports car? Am I an astronaut?"

Eric laughed. And then he realized I wasn't entirely joking.

"You're... well, you're happy!"

"Come on, tell me."

"I really need to focus on this."

One thing that I still had on Eric was size and speed. Before he could stop me, I was across the room, holding his math book above his head.

"Tell me," I demanded.

"Come on, stop being a jerk." He jumped to get his book back, and I lifted it just out of his reach.

"Tell me and you can have your book back."

"I lowered the book, just above his outstretched fingers, and as he jumped, I pulled it back up. I couldn't help it. I laughed. I knew I was being mean, but it was as close to a game we had played since he had changed. Looking back on it, I can see why Eric said what he did next. He was frustrated. Here he was, trying to work hard to get ahead, and everyone in our family was giving him grief.

"You want to know? You really want to know? Alright, I'll tell you, in the future you work at that stupid store with Dad. You're a loser. You have a wife. She's a loser. And you have two kids, who, when I am not bailing their asses out of trouble in school, are usually flunking most of their classes. You hate your life but aren't even brave enough to admit it because that would mean changing something. The highlight of your week is when I take you out for drinks and you get so piss drunk you can forget, for just a few hours, how fucking miserable your life is."

I let the book sink to his level, and the words washed over me. Snatching the book, Eric stomped over to the bed and pulled the blankets over himself. I stood there, not sure what to do or say. I wanted to hit him so bad, make him feel as small and dumb as I did right now. But even under the covers, he was still just a little kid. After what seemed like years passed, I finally moved toward the door to leave.

"I'm sorry," Eric said. "I didn't mean that."

I didn't say anything.

"Your wife, Tina, she's really nice. You meet her in high school. Your kids... well... at least I won't have them in class now..." he laughed trying to cut the tension down. It was the most grownup thing I had seen him do yet. "And if it means anything, I always look forward to our Friday nights."

"You're wrong," I said at last.

"About what," Eric said as he pulled back the covers.

"You aren't sorry. And you meant every word. But, hey, that is exactly the kind of stuff Dad says after he talks to Mom."

Eric didn't say anything.

"Good night," I said. And then I left his room.

Eric moved out at the end of the next month. I think he talked to someone to speed it up. We would see him from time to time, whenever he could find time in his busy schedule to come home and visit. Despite the puncture of the space time whatever, my future turned out a lot like Eric said. I went through school, met Tina, and started working at the tire shop with Dad. But I ended up with three kids, not two. Fluctuations to the timeline, I guess.

Finally, one Christmas, Eric pulled me aside and started talking excitedly. "Hey, I think I'm going to go through with it again!"

"What are you talking about?"

"You know, time travel!"

"Why would you want to do that?" I asked. "Aren't you happy with your job at the Justice Department?"

"Oh, I love my job and everything, but if I go back again this time I'll be able to really get a leg up on law school. Maybe start my own practice, serve on the court... hell, I may even get a chance to start a family like you and Tina."

I looked at my wife with our third daughter. She was sitting on the floor as the baby toddled around her laughing.

"It's like you said, buddy, anything is possible. You just have to work hard enough at it."

"I never said that."

"Sure you said it all the time... oh... right. You said it on our Friday nights out."

"Well, that never happened for me buddy."

"Right. Sorry." He was quiet for a little longer. "I guess I just need a way to break it to Mom."

"Good luck," I said as I walked back into the living room.

Eric didn't invite any of us to his second time jump. I wondered if we had gone the first time? In any regard, it didn't really impact us too much. He had never really been around after he had moved out. But I can't help but think about him sometimes. Especially what it would be like to do as he has done. Jumping back again and again to get ahead further and further. But I know it won't ever happen for me.

Instead, I just watch my children's faces, worrying that one day their expressions will glass over, and what I thought was permanent will be brushed away, as they begin remembering things I have never known.

LAUNCH PAD

It is sunny. The Earth is still alive, but those who know, know that it is on life support.

The stage is set for a festive announcement, nonetheless.

Balloons, leaking helium but still buoyant, float about.

A woman in a sharp suit steps forward, adjusts the mic and begins to speak.

"My fellow citizens, today I am proud to be among you, to count you as my friends and peers, because today is the day we relaunch our too long dormant space program. More than a century from the time our ancestors walked on the moon, and several decades from when my father, a pilot himself, brought me to this place to watch the final ship launch, we are taking the much-needed step of reigniting our space program!

Clap, clap, clap.

For too long, we have allowed the most divisive voices among us to dictate the policies of our future. War, disease, unethical AI, all of it has left our world broken.

Mumble, mumble, mumble.

"Amen!" an older woman standing in the front of the crowd shouts out.

"With this new space field, here in the heart of Ohio, we pump needed vitality back into the dreams of those who would dare for a better future!"

The journalists covering the story, some robot, others human, take notes.

Cliché, cliché, cliché.

"BORING!" One writer reports to their site *The Daily Bully*.

"Relaunch Fails to Launch," writes another for the *Atlantic*.

"The Senator made several good points about the spaceships. Surely this is historic," the robotic journalist produces. It uploads the story to the *New York Times*.

"Now, I know there are those who deride this decision, economically costly yes, but what they just don't get is you cannot put a price on dreams. It may be divisive to say, but there are those who would rather cater to religious zealots sitting in their cathedrals than deal with the problems we face with real solutions."

Clap, clap, clap.

The audience, all supporters of the Senator, agree.

"Senator doubles down on divisive rhetoric," one journalist reports. They upload it to *XPost*.

"Can't We Just All Be Friends?" a writer for a local news outlet writes.

"The Presidential Campaign Trail Continues to Offer Splendid Choices to Voters: Click to see the 10

Top Reasons You Should VOTE!" the robot journalist uploads to *ABC*.

"You know folks, my time in office has not been easy."

Murmur, murmur, murmur.

"The wars abroad and those coming home to us have already started to take a toll."

Shaking heads, shaking heads, nod in agreement, nod in agreement.

"My brother was killed just two years ago in the Texas uprising and thank god the Mexican government was able to intervene to help us stop that cruel and vicious insurrection."

"COMMUNISM!!!!" the robot journalist uploads an instantaneous 900-word story to *Fox*.

"If we continue down the way that many would have us go, then we could see war rip apart our cities, our nation, and destroy long time alliances with other countries. It is why, aside from being here today to celebrate the re-opening of this space field, I am launching my bid to be the next President of these United States."

CLAP, CLAP, CLAP. WHIIISSSTTTTLLLLEEEEE.

"YEAH!!!!" supporters yell.

The journalists begin recording and uploading in a frenzy.

The robot reporter loses connection to the internet. Looking about, it sees two journalists have a hot spot on their phone. Checking to make sure they have accepted the terms and conditions, the robot reporter jumps onto their Wi-Fi, pushing them off in the process.

"What Does This Mean for the Future?" it reports to one outlet. 500 words.

"Will the Senator Trounce Her Opponents?" another story. 500 words.

"What Would You Look Like Running for Office? Upload Your Photo and Find Out!" 200 words with a link embedded. The filter it uses is the stage the Senator is standing on, the airfield behind it. The Senator continues her speech, behind her the once abandoned field awaits what will be built.

"My fellow Americans, I promise you this. If elected, we will win this race to the stars. This will not become a planet of ghosts."

Clap, clap, clap.

Cliché, cliché, cliché.

Click, click, click as the news stories get published, read, and shared.

SPARKY IS A GOOD BOY

My name is Sparky. I am an agent for the Collective. I am trying to be a very good agent because the mission of the collective is quite important. The Collective exists to save as many people as possible from the ending of the world! The ending of the world is bad. But the Collective is saving people from it. That is why the Collective is good and important.

My mission is to help a very important Man agree to join the Collective. So far, the Man has been reluctant to join us. This is odd to me because the Collective is good, and the end of the world is bad, and if the Man does not join the Collective, he will die! This would be bad. The other agents have told me we will leave for our mission shortly. I will make another entry when I can.

END ENTRY— AGENT SPARKY

The Man is not happy I am here. This is odd. After traveling many hours in a car (I like this) we arrived at the Man's home. He has converted a corn silo into his offices. The Man is a writer and inventor. The Man is one of the first time travelers ever! This is very important. The Man is very important.

When we arrived, he came out of his home with a gun! This was not good.

The other agents, two nice people named Barbara and Jeremy, raised their hands and spoke rapidly. Before the Man could do anything else Barbara opened the back door, and I jumped out! I was ready to run because I had been in the car so long, and also because the Man had a gun!

"What the actual fuck," the Man said. (This is a bad word).

"That is a bad word," I told the Man.

He looked at me surprised, then at the two agents.

"So, it's true, you have figured out how to make them talk."

"The Earth is ending Eric Lewis. It would be wrong to leave them behind, and it would be equally wrong to just force them on a ship like Noah's ark. They need to have a choice in the matter. Sparky here has not only chosen to join the Collective, he has also volunteered to be an agent and help convince others, like yourself, to save themselves."

The Man then pointed his gun at me. I whined, laid on the ground and buried my head in the grass. This was very upsetting.

The Man then sighed and walked back into his home, slamming the door.

The other agents talked to me then for a few moments. Was I sure I wanted this mission, it would be alright, they said, if I decided to leave.

NO! I said this so strongly that I barked as well as communicated via my voice implant (I love this implant; it turns thoughts into words!).

"You are a good boy, Sparky," Agent Jeremy said.

I wagged my tail then. I am a good boy indeed!

END ENTRY— AGENT SPARKY

I spent all night outside the Man's home. In the morning, when he came out, he groaned to see me laying in front of his door.

"Good morning!" I barked and said with words. "I am hungry. Are you hungry? If you are hungry, we should eat food."

"You are not eating any of my food, you stupid mutt."

The Man stepped over me and began walking away toward his corn silo.

"The other agents feared you would not want to share food, so I have brought my own."

I had found a nice place to hide my case of food. It was programmed to open only for my barks.

"But we can eat together!"

The Man said nothing, and I followed a safe distance behind him asking him questions about his work.

"Is it true you developed the technology that makes the Collective possible?"

"Is it true you regret this invention?"

"Why do you regret this?"

"Are you not worried that you will hurt when the world ends, and you die?"

The Man got to the corn silo and slammed the door in my face!

At this moment, I realized this may be a very, very hard mission.

I sat outside the door and whined to be let in. This did not work.

I said, "Can I please come in? I need to tell you about the benefits of the Collective. I cannot do this if you do not listen!"

These pleas did not work either.

I hated to do what I did next, but I had no choice. It felt wrong, something I had not done since I was a very young puppy, before the Collective had helped me gain language and thought, but this was desperate. I had only three days to convince the Man. After that, I would join the Collective, and we would begin preparations to leave the Earth forever.

I began to bark. I barked very loudly. Many humans do not realize how much dogs can bark, as their voices grow tired very quickly. But dogs, we can bark for very long! It is a matter of making your voice run a long chase. I think most humans, even those who talk a lot, talk too much like humans. Run for a time, stop, run some more, walk, rest. Run some more. Dogs run much faster, stronger, and for longer distances. Our voices can fall into that running.

Bark. Bark. Bark. Bark.

I began to jump up and down and run about the corn silo to make sure my barks made their way in.

Bark. Bark. Bark.

This fit the pattern of chasing a rabbit. Rabbits are fast, but dogs are stronger. I do not chase rabbits now; in fact, I have convinced some to join the Collective. But before my changes, I chased many.

Bark. Bark. Bark.

After this series of barks, I sat threw my head back and howled as loudly as I could.

Normally, howls are for long distance communicating, but it was appropriate here. I imagined the Man sitting alone in his corn silo and let the howl change to match the pitch of his voice. I called to him, JOIN US!, I said in that howl. DO NOT STAY ALONE! WE ARE YOUR FRIENDS AND FAMILY! WE LOVE YOU!

HOOOOOOOOOOOOOOOOOWWWWWWWWWWWWWWWLLLLLLLLLLL!

"Jesus Fucking Christ," the Man yelled opening the door. "Do you ever shut the fuck up!"

"No," I said, "not when I have a mission!"

I was wagging my tail, and my tongue was panting now.

"Can I please come in?"

"Only if you promise to be quiet!"

"Yes!" I said padding softly into his corn silo. "I will not be as loud."

Inside the corn silo, there were stacks and stacks of papers, books, models for inventions.

I barked excitedly and jumped in the air before zooming in a circle.

"You said you'd be quiet," the Man yelled.

"I apologize. I am just very impressed. I see why the Collective wants you to join us!"

"I am never going to join that god forsaken computer program," the Man said.

He walked over to his desk and sat down.

I walked over to him after a moment and sat.

"Why?"

"Why do you care?" the Man asked without looking at me.

"Because the Earth is dying, those who do not join a ship will die with it. I do not like it when things die, so I do not want you to stay. Because you will die."

I whined at the thought.

"Everything dies mutt."

"Yes, but we can sometimes choose when and where. This is nice."

The Man said nothing.

"For example, I had a brother, he grew up on a neighboring farm from me (I diverged and told him my pedigree history. My family had been lucky that three of us lived on neighboring farms. I was able to see my mother and brother and sister regularly. My other sisters I never got to meet. This was common before animals could be changed. Another reason the Collective is good!)

"And my brother CHOSE not to fight that bull in the connecting field. If he had, he probably would have died. So, he chose to live! This is good."

The Man put his project down and looked at me.

"You poor, sad, mongrel," he said.

I titled my head in confusion.

The Man understood the gesture and explained further.

"You were born a dog, an honest to god dog, and the perverts at the Collective turned you into.... this," he gestured at me.

"I do not understand," I said.

"Dogs aren't supposed to be able to talk. They took you and sliced you open and did all kinds of procedures on you. Now you talk and think like this. You aren't a dog, and you aren't a human. You are a freak."

I said nothing for a moment.

"That was not very nice to say," I barked to add emphasis.

"Well, I am not a nice man," he said.

I laid down. I watched the man work.

END ENTRY— AGENT SPARKY

I am now at the end of the second day of my mission. It is not going well. The first day ended after the Man left his corn silo and stomped back to his house. I spent the night outside again. I ate my meal and listened to the forest surrounding the Man's house.

I am sad to see so much of this die. It is dying. You can smell it if you are paying attention. The other animals are in flight. Birds are not sure where to go. Larger animals are agitated. I heard a bear rumble through the trees at one point. The bear will be important later in this entry.

The next day the Man came stomping back out of his home, but instead of going to the corn silo, he walked off into the woods. I followed at a safe distance, close enough for him to hear me but not too close.

"Where are we going?" I asked.

"We aren't going anywhere. I am going somewhere; you are just following."

"Where are you going?" I corrected.

The Man did not answer.

I sniffed the air. The bear from the night before was not far, but not close enough for alarm. I used my computer implant to run a background watch. If the bear came closer, I would warn the Man. I did not want her to hurt him. The bear from what I could smell was in serious distress. Hungry, angry, and looking for a reason to fight something that threatened her.

After a half an hour of walking, the man stopped by a sharp drop in the land. Water from a stream poured over the lip and fell to the ground below. It was very far down.

"I do not like heights," I said.

"No one wants you here, so you can leave."

I sat stubbornly down. I am a good boy. I am a good agent. I would not abandon my mission.

The Man set up a recording device and then relaxed beside it.

After another half an hour, the Man stood, stretched, and let out a deep sigh. Then he collected his recording equipment and began the trek back to his home.

"Why did you do that?" I asked.

The Man did not answer.

"Are you trying to save things before the end of the world?" I asked again.

Again, the Man said nothing.

This was getting me nowhere. I thought for several minutes as I followed behind the Man. I even resorted to looking through the Collective's files. This is not forbidden, but it is something that is difficult to do. Accessing the beings residing in the Collective (there are thousands and thousands of lifeforms stored there) removes your attention from your body and surroundings.

I spoke with several psychologists about the Man's behaviors. I also spoke with a family of squirrels I had recruited. Finally, one of my good friends Cheddar offered insight.

"This Man sounds very odd. He helped create the Collective?"

"Yes," I said.

Cheddar thought for a few moments.

"Have you asked him why he dislikes what he created?"

"I have asked him several things, but not this. The other agents who brought me here did not elaborate."

Together, Cheddar and I moved through the Collective to the human agents and sifted through their memories about the Man. There was both much there and nothing of use. The Man was considered a brilliant scientist. He had helped lay the groundwork for a more ethical download of life. Before the Man, there was a constant worry about how cruel it could be to confine a living being to a computer. The Man had changed that, liberated it, now living beings could end their existence without the aid of someone outside the program. The living beings could also reform the space they digitally lived in. These were all good things.

"I do not understand," Cheddar said.

"I do not either."

"You need to ask him, and if he is not willing to share, then maybe just accept he is odd and does not want to live."

At that point, the alarms in my implants began to blare. Pulling myself from the Collective, I knew the bear was dangerously close.

I froze but the Man continued to walk.

"STOP!" I barked.

The Man spun around startled.

"What are you going on about?"

He could not hear the bear, or smell her, but would soon see.

"There is a bear very close, she is very angry, she will do us harm."

The Man looked about frantically.

"Where?"

I did not have a chance to answer. The bear came bursting over the near hill. She was moving so quick that the Man had no chance of outrunning her. I could, of course, and would be aided by the fact that the Man would be between her and me.

The Man fumbled through his bag looking for something to use as a weapon.

I readied my body and as the bear drew close launched myself between the two.

I barked very good. I growled even better. I showed my teeth.

The bear slowed and growled back.

I am not a very big dog, part beagle. But I am not as small as Cheddar who is a chihuahua. I know how to fight!

Bark, bark, bark!

GROOOOOOOOOOWWWWLLLLLLLLL.

The bear was estimating how best to kill me. The Man behind me was frantic.

"Run!" I said to the Man. "Run, now!"

"But, what about you?"

I turned on the Man and lunged to scare him.

The Man was not expecting this and began to run as fast as he could.

I am proud to say I learned this trick from a book called White Fang! You pretend to be angry and scare the one you are protecting or love away. I do not love the Man, but I am protecting him. I turned back to the bear. She attempted to follow the Man, estimating he would be easier to kill. I launched between them again and snapped my jaws at her.

The bear reared up on her two hind legs before pouncing at me.

I jumped back.

I am not big, but I am fast!

The bear and I did this for nearly an hour. I would run behind the bear and snap at her hind quarters. By the time she had turned around, I would be zooming off into the forest only to double back and repeat the process. I accessed several files on how to fight a bear. This helped. The Collective is good!

Finally, the bear began to tire. The poor thing was so exhausted already. The planet was dying; there was not enough food.

When she sat down in defeat, I padded around her sniffing the air.

The whole time this had been happening I had been asking the Collective to judge if she should be invited to join us.

It was unanimous, yes.

My collar released the small drone, and it launched itself into the back of the head of the bear. She was so tired she barely made a sound.

Slowly the tiny robots released themselves into her, building structures to help her think and speak.

"I... I... what is this?"

"Hello," I said. "My name is Sparky. I am an agent of the Collective."

The bear and I sat together for another hour as the process completed itself.

"And you see," I said completing the download, "this is why the Collective was established. We would die with the Earth if we did not leave, but we are trying to give as many life forms as possible the choice."

"Everyone gets a choice?" she asked.

"No," and I whined to emphasize how sad this was. "We do not have the time or agents needed to gather everyone."

"This is not fair!" the bear said.

"I agree."

"Who... who brought you into the Collective?"

I explained how my mother had been volunteered for the project by her humans. Once she had the consciousness necessary, she demanded my siblings and I be given the same opportunity.

"My babies are dead," the bear said. "They could not survive without food."

"I am very sorry."

"What happens to us now?"

"You have a choice. You can reject this technology and go back to your previous state and stay on the planet, or you can join us and leave and find a new life!"

The bear said she would think about it, accessing the files of the Collective she knew how long she had before it would be too late to request an agent to come and retrieve her.

"Thank you, Sparky," she said getting up to leave.

"Thank you," I replied. "I hope you join us in the Collective. Then you can pick a name, and I can call you this name, and we can be better friends!"

She left then to contemplate her future.

It is late now. I will finish this entry in the morning.

END ENTRY, AGENT SPARKY

When I returned to the Man's house after the incident with the bear, the Man was amazed to find me still alive.

"I thought you would be bear food for sure!"

"Thank you for worrying! I am fine. I am an agent of the Collective and am well trained."

The Man welcomed me in his home then, and I was relieved to finally be making progress. The home was very cozy. I found a nice rug to lay on and did so. I was very tired from the bear.

The Man asked me about my history, and I told him everything he wanted to know. I explained I was one of the best agents of the Collective and had recruited many members.

I lied to the Man about the bear though. I did not want to let him know she had been changed. This might upset him. He seemed happier thinking we had fought, although I know he knew I could not kill a bear! Therefore, my lie to him was not as bad, I think, because he was already lying to himself.

After I had told him my story, I asked Cheddar's question.

"Why do you hate the Collective?"

The Man sat quietly for a long time, then said, "I can't explain it, but I can show you. Tomorrow. Tomorrow, I will show you."

He gave me food then and a bowl of water and went to bed.

I fell asleep very quickly after that. I allowed my consciousness to split from my body so it could rest and went and found the bear to continue talking to her. She was nestled under her favorite tree.

"Hello, Sparky," she said.

"Hello," I answered.

I could see what she was seeing, hear what she was hearing, and smell all her nose detected.

"Have you decided on a name?"

"Yes."

"Can I know what it is?"

She showed me her two cubs who had died that season, the memory smelled like pine since that is where she liked to keep them. The needles muffled the sound of them, kept them safe.

"My name is Two Pine," she said.

"That is a lovely name."

"Thank you."

"Good night, Two Pine! If you have anything you need let me know. I am not far away."

The Man is awake now and wants me to come with him. Will update entry later.

END ENTRY, AGENT SPARKY

I am waiting for the agents to come and retrieve me.

I have succeeded! They will continue to think I am a good boy.

The Man drove me from his home in the woods into the nearby town. As we drove, he explained much. How he had gone to university and learned about computer programming and philosophy, how he and many others had come to realize the planet was dying. How no matter how many time travelers returned to this moment the outcome kept repeating itself.

"I and others figured out we needed a new way to be, if we could just understand each other, then maybe we could either save the world, or at least, begin the foundations of a new one."

The Man had travelled back in time five times to continue his work. It was so complicated to build the technology of the Collective that no one lifetime could achieve it.

"Would you, Sparky, ever go back in time?"

"No," I answered. "My mind requires computers implanted in my body. If I went back to a time before that, I would not exist."

I did not add that the Man, like all humans, were very fortunate to be able to time travel. It was a privilege many life forms did not have. I think he would have been angry if I said privilege.

We finally arrived at our destination. It was a parking lot behind the local city hall.

"Why are we here?" I asked.

"Look, what do you see?"

"I see a parking lot. I see a recycling bin. I see where some squirrels have made their home in that abandoned building across the street."

I could have continued that I smelled even more. Humans outside of the Collective often forget that for many of us "seeing" is more than sight. The Man was definitely one of those who would not remember that others "saw" in different ways.

"I will tell you what I see," the Man said. "I see futility. Do you know what futility is dog?"

I looked up at him.

"I have access to many words, so yes. The dictionary is good. I like the dictionary. Futility is a good word to describe a sad situation."

"Exactly."

He opened the back of his car and retrieved the can of kerosine he had brought. Walking up to the recycling bin, he began to dump the kerosine all over it. I watched, cocking my head to the side and whining in worry. This was very dangerous. Kerosine also smells very bad. I do not like it.

When the Man had finished, he pulled out his lighter and threw it into the bin. It exploded in fire. The smell was even worse now.

The Man went back to his car. I stared at the fire for a few more minutes before joining. The Man then began to drive back to his home as the sound of firetrucks could be heard barreling to the scene.

"Why did you do that?" I asked.

"Because the earth is dead. It doesn't matter how much you fucking recycle. It doesn't matter how many times I or anyone else go back in time. It doesn't fucking matter how many people and animals and shit plants you pack into your collective. We are all fucked."

I yawned then. Yawns in humans can mean boredom. Yawns for dogs mean stress. I was very stressed. I had failed to convince the Man to join the Collective. Also, I did not like him. I felt very complicated. I was glad he had helped create the Collective because the Collective is good! But I did not like him and did not want him to join. I was secretly glad he would be staying here, that he would die, and that I would not speak to him ever again. This made me feel bad. These were bad thoughts. I, Sparky, was being a bad boy.

When we got back to his home, I exited the car and trotted off to where my case of food was. The Man watched me as, case handle in mouth, I trotted past him.

"That it? No goodbye?"

"Goodbye. Thank you for your work on the Collective. I am leaving now."

I made my way far down the road to a place where cars could pull off. I would wait here. I did not want to be near the Man anymore.

"Sparky?" a voice said to me through the Collective.

"Yes," I said my ears perking. I could use a companion at this moment.

"It is Two Pine. I have made my decision."

We spoke for a few more minutes, and I gave her my location. Against my will, my tail began to wag. Through the Collective, I reached out to the agents to come and get me and to bring a larger vehicle. We had succeeded. We had saved one more.

HOPE SPRINGS

CONTINUED...

"Hey, Haruko! Over here!" Gabriel Virenhal shouted. Stepping over the rubble, Haruko made their way towards the voice.

"What is it?" they asked as they set their metal case down. The sun was hot, and that, combined with the dust from the collapsed buildings, made the air heavy and uncomfortable. "Did you find something?" They wiped the sweat off their brow and looked over their colleague's shoulder.

"We got a survivor in here," Gabriel answered as they swept their detector over the jagged pieces of metal and concrete. Listening through the headphones, they nodded their head. "Definitely have a survivor. Get the rods ready."

"Give me that," Haruko said as they took the headphones. Listening to the static, they barely made out the faint calls for help. "You have to be kidding me, Gabriel. They're a goner."

"That's not for us to decide. You know that. Now get the rod ready."

Sighing, Haruko pulled out a glowing green rod from the case. "How far down do you suppose they are?"

Gabriel took the headphones back and listened. "Ten feet. Maybe more. Hurry he doesn't have much time left."

In the blink of an eye, Haruko and Gabriel were ten feet under the collapsed building.

Haruko twisted and turned, trying to see in the dingy light. "You'd think the people in this era would learn how to build a damn building. Especially if they're going to live in a part of the world prone to earthquakes."

Haruko had never fully understood these past periods, so much so that they still questioned their decision to join the New Gem City's time travelling mission. Sure, there was all the talk back home about how they were building hope for people stuck in the past, but sympathizing with people in the abstract, and helping them in the concrete were two different things. Especially when so many of the disasters were the people's own making. These earthquakes were just the beginning of it. If humanity kept it up, this earth would be torn apart all over again.

"Stop complaining and give me that," Gabriel said, gesturing towards the glowing rod. Haruko passed it to their outstretched hands. Even though they were only a few feet from each other, Haruko could barely see them.

"Why are you breathing so hard?" Haruko asked. "Are you alright?"

"It's not me," Gabriel responded.

Haruko stared into the dark harder.

"Oh, my god..." Haruko said as their eyes finally adjusted.

A small bleeding child, a boy Haruko would guess, lay directly in front of them. His face was smeared with blood and dirt. It was difficult to make out distinct features, but one thing did catch their attention. One arm lay at an awkward angle, the other clutched something in a tight fist.

"Here we go," Gabriel said. They made a copy of the boy's mind with the rod, digitally downloaded him, and readjusted the settings so he would feel comfort, hope. Gabriel ran this simulation for months, and then, gently placed the copy of the conscious back into the boy's mind.

"There we go. Good as new." Gabriel announced.

Haruko watched as the boy's breathing deepened. Slowly, his eyes fluttered open.

"Hurry," Gabriel said, "let's get out of here."

But before Haruko could move, the boy woke and looked directly at them.

"Ki ou?" he asked.

"Me? Oh, I'm nobody," Haruko answered instinctively.

"Haruko, what the hell are you doing? Stop talking to them and move!"

One instant Gabriel was glaring at them, the next they was gone.

Haruko started to follow, but the boy spoke again.

"Manman? Manman?" He then asked if Haruko was an angel?

Looking at his clenched fist, Haruko saw what he was holding. It took all their will power not to vomit. A hand, attached to nothing but the pieces of concrete was grasped tightly by the boy.

"I'm not your mother," Haruko answered nearly choking. Then, unable to think of anything else, she said, "Don't give up hope, kid."

"Manman, ede m'! Manman!"

Haruko disappeared, but not before they heard the boy begin to cry.

"How many times do I need to remind you, don't talk to past people!" Gabriel was walking as fast as they could, kicking the stones in front of them in aggravation.

Haruko followed behind, metal case swinging in one hand. Haruko smacked their overalls with their free hand, desperately trying to remove the dirt from their clothes.

"I can't help it," Haruko said. "Sometimes they just see me." Haruko knew that was a lie. They were just being uncareful. No one in the past could see them, except in those few moments when the downloads were taking place.

"I can't ignore them," Haruko said, "It feels wrong to replenish their hopes and then just leave."

Gabriel spun around. "At what point did it become important as to how you 'felt' about it? Hmm? This world is on the brink of figuring out time travel. You know what that means?"

"Yes," Haruko answered.

"Really, because I don't think you do. Once these people in this period learn time travel, they will figure out only how to travel into the past, and it won't just be their consciousnesses. Their bodies. Entire machines. Armies if they want."

"Yep." Haruko said looking about and trying to ignore Gabriel's lecture.

"*Yep*? Well, Haruko Jones III, let me ask you what happens once the people in this time do know time travel, and there are reports of strange 'angels' showing up left and right with advanced technology? Don't you think they might put two and two together and figure out that they are being visited from the future? What do you think the odds are they go looking for us?"

Haruko said nothing.

"Yeah, that's what I thought. There are misogynistic socio-paths in this time who would love, just love, to know that humanity's descendants are walking about on another planet, and that, if they just knew the coordinates, could pop in from the past to pay us a visit."

Haruko finally spoke to defend themself. "Let it happen, is what I say. We will kick their asses back to Earth."

"Oh, really, a war? Do you really want dead soldiers of Earth's past reactionary armies haunting generations of New Gem City?" Gabriel screwed their face into a scowl. "Haruko, you know where my last name comes from?"

"Yes, of course."

"Do you really? My forefather fucking enslaved people. He gave us all his last name. A version of him is prancing about on this planet, a hell of a lot more alive then his ghost back home, and he is a media celebrity just itching to become a warlord. When will it happen? Who knows! But in any case, it's not good. What if he tries to get back to us?"

Haruko didn't say anything. As the silence grew, Haruko noticed where they were. Gunfire and explosions could be heard in the distance, growing louder by the minute.

"I hate this war," Haruko muttered. They had heard endless stories about it from the veterans back home.

"Yeah. So, do I. So does everyone back in New Gem City," Gabriel answered. "But Haruko, do it again Haruko, let yourself be seen, on purpose or by accident, and I'll report you."

Gabriel put their headphones on and began to walk towards the gunfire. Haruko readjusted their grip on the metal case and followed.

Before long, they were in the middle of the fighting. Bullets whizzed past as Gabriel calmly scanned the area. Haruko wandered around, moving the remains of a smoldering car door with the toe of their boot. They knew the bullets couldn't harm them, but they were annoying, like biting flies on a summer day. Two went through Haruko's shoulder, as another cut through their ear. Haruko swatted at them in impatience.

"Do you have anything yet?" Haruko asked.

Gabriel passed the scanner over the area once again.

Haruko was about to complain some more, when Gabriel said, "Over that way. It doesn't look like they have much of a chance, but they're refusing to give up."

Gabriel began to run, and Haruko trying to keep up, followed. The case began to swing as Haruko went faster and faster. A bullet suddenly went through their right hand. It agitated Haruko's skin nearly causing them to drop the case. With their left hand, they grabbed the bottom, keeping it from falling.

That was close, Haruko thought. Too close.

A few moments later, Gabriel and Haruko were standing among three soldiers. One was sitting in the corner of the bombed out building, holding his head and crying. The other two were against the far wall. Haruko walked towards the one crying.

"Leave 'em," Gabriel called. "He's already given up hope. There's nothing we can do for him now."

Haruko looked at the bawling soldier. Haruko hesitated for a moment, before turning back towards Gabriel.

"Alright, what we got?"

"This guy," Gabriel pointed to one of the soldiers against the wall, "has three bullets lodged in his stomach and is bleeding badly. But he hasn't given up, yet. Get the downloader ready."

Haruko looked at the third soldier. He was continuing to shoot, yelling encouragement to his dying friend.

"What about this one," Haruko asked as they handed the device to Gabriel.

Gabriel sat the rod down carefully, and scanned the soldier in question.

"Are you kidding? Any more hope and this guy would be manic." Gabriel touched the back of the wounded man and opened his mind. As Haruko looked at the wounded soldier, they realized he wasn't a man.

"He's just a boy," Haruko said.

"What was that?" Gabriel asked as they removed the depleted hope. Looking at the boy, Gabriel agreed. "Yeah, all of them are pretty young. This is Chicago right before the total collapse. Its spooky as hell being here after hearing all the stories back home."

Gabriel adjusted the controls, so the soldier's download would begin the process of healing. Gently, as the process ended, Gabriel reinserted the consciousness into the boy. Haruko took the now empty downloader and was getting ready to place back in the case when the wounded boy's eyes fluttered open.

"Haruko! You're in his line of vision, move!"

But it was too late. The soldier had seen them and began to yell.

Before Haruko could move, the soldier kicked wildly.

Even though there was no chance he could hurt them, Haruko acted out of instinct. Leaning back, Haruko fell.

"NO!" Gabriel yelled as they stood and tried to hold the soldier back.

Haruko landed on their back. The metal case slipped from Haruko's grasp, crashing beside them. A sharp pain shot through their ribs—phantom pain, they knew, but still it caught her breath. The soldier scrambled up, one hand clutching his bleeding stomach.

"Stop him!" Gabriel yelled.

Haruko fumbled for a device, any device, in their bag, but Gabriel was already moving. In one fluid motion, they pressed their palm against the boy's temple, initiating a rapid neural dampening. His eyes rolled back, and he slumped to the ground.

They stood in the silence of aftermath. Haruko could still hear the wailing soldier in the corner. He hadn't stopped crying.

"We're going to have to purge this zone," Gabriel said quietly, wiping her hands. "This whole sector. Anyone who saw or heard anything."

Haruko sat up, her face ashen. "You mean... everyone?"

Gabriel didn't answer. The boy had seen their technology, gotten too good of a look at them. There was no mistaking them for anything other than what they were— two people with impossible technology.

Haruko stared at the boy still crying, the other still firing.

They packed the case in silence. The scanner blinked once. Twice. Green lit for the sweep. Before leaving, Gabriel turned back. The soldier who had cried through it all was still in the corner. He looked at her. Their eyes met. This time, Gabriel didn't look away.

They knelt beside him and handed him something small—a memory node, a sliver of light. Not the full download. Just enough to make him remember how it felt to believe in tomorrow.

Haruko watched.

As the soldier blinked, stunned by the gentle warmth now blooming inside his mind, Gabriel stood and joined Haruko.

They disappeared just as the bomb fell.

Haruko sat in the waiting room at the hospital. They adjusted the bracelet on their left hand. No matter how much they tried, they couldn't get the piece of metal to fit comfortably.

"Is this really necessary?" they had asked the New Gem City's representative.

"Apparently so," they answered as they clamped and locked the bracelet on Haruko's wrist. Now, even if they wanted to, Haruko could not be seen by anyone from this time and was stuck in this period until the governor's office in New Gem City decided what to do. Most likely a trial. Haruko's actions had led to three deaths, deaths that should not have occurred. It was a humiliating new low for Haruko. Only the biggest screw ups weren't trusted with their own visibility and time movement.

"Hey," Gabriel said as they sat down beside Haruko.

"Hey, yourself," Haruko said as they leaned their head back.

"How are you doing?"

"Other than being stuck in a place with horrible food, uncomfortable chairs, old magazines, and a television that only plays CNN Health, I'm great. Oh, wait. I forgot to mention that my case is under review, and I'll probably be court martialed."

"Court martial... that is a harsh term. I mean, at worst, you just get expelled and get to go home and be a civilian. And at least they put you somewhere... happy?" Gabriel offered.

Gabriel and Haruko watched as people, mostly men, but a few families sat and waited impatiently. Every so often a doctor would emerge from the doors and tell the family one of two things. "It's a boy," or "It's a girl." Always, "Congratulations!"

"Medieval gender constructs," Haruko said. "And it's easy for you to say being remanded back is no big deal. You know what my parents are going to say? I am named after one of the martyrs of the colony, they'll say. Should have done better, they'll say."

Gabriel scratched the side of their face thinking. "Yeah, well, you'll be the talk of the town for sure. Probably all three cities, really."

They watched as a doctor walked out and spoke to a man.

"Really," he said smiling. "When do I get to see her?"

"Just follow me," the doctor answered.

"If it means anything," Gabriel said after a few minutes, "I told them in my report you tried to save that kid."

"Did you also mention how careless I was, letting myself be seen?"

Gabriel didn't say anything.

"You know what, screw this," Haruko said as they stood. One moment they were standing in the delivery room, the next Haruko was on a hill looking down at a rescue crew.

"Are you completely nuts?" Gabriel asked as they appeared. "You're not supposed to leave your designated detention area. They stripped you of time travel, but they'll limit your ability to move about altogether if you keep it up."

"What are they going to do," Haruko asked. They held up her wrist and shook the bracelet. "Punish me?"

Gabriel shook their head. They looked around and then back at Haruko.

"Where are we?"

The sound of the emergency vehicles answered. They were racing to a school building. Gabriel had seen plenty of these. Another mass shooting.

"What do you think his chances are?" Haruko asked.

"Say what?" Gabriel asked.

"The boy we replenished before the incident with the soldiers. What do you think his chances are he'll be alright?"

"Haruko," Gabriel said, "why do you do this to yourself?"

"We go around these periods, giving people hope, and sometimes I can't help but wonder, what's the point? Are we really helping, or are we just being cruel? Why should we give hope to people when we know what is going to happen next? Most of these people are going to perish in the coming— fuck the ongoing— burning of this planet. Why not do the humane thing and let them end their misery?"

Below them they could see parents frantically arriving at the school. They were met by a barricade of police as they demanded to be let in and save their children.

"Haruko, listen to me," Gabriel said as they turned to her friend. "Hope is important. It's a form of faith. In turn faith is a kind of love. And love, besides being a form of hope, is the only thing that promises to make this world better. Take that away and you might as well destroy not just the planet, but everyone on it and after. Imagine that waiting room we were just in. All of those new people lying in beds, ready to move into the world. Every problem humanity faces is always only one generation away from solution."

"Doesn't matter anyway," Haruko said.

"Don't give up just yet," Gabriel said. "Who knows, maybe this plan will help save more people, restore hope just enough to get more people on the ships to a new start."

Together the two turned back to the school, where gun fire could still be heard, where screaming of parents and sirens could still be heard, where all of it could be heard for a day and into an unforgetting future.

FLOOD WATERS

The year is 2004. The beginning of the cycle of the universe is so distant in the past that (save for a few beings) it is nothing but a speculation. It is so far removed from the end of this cycle that no single being in the universe has even begun to contemplate it.

This is a "bedrock" timeline, as time travelers will come to call it. These are timelines that have yet to experience time travel and with it the rewrites and edits and alterations that follow.

Eventually, this will all come to pass.

In roughly five years, the timeline will rupture with possibility, and time trekkers and robots and multi-timeline generational spaceships will come. But right now, at this point, two people sit on a couch watching the evening news.

"This is horrible," the woman says.

"Hmmm mmm," the man says.

They are married, have been for ten years at this point. They are still madly in love, have no children, and are quite happy with the decision— despite being told by their parents, grandparents, and friends with children they will change their minds or come to regret the decision in later life.

"No one will carry on your name," the man's mother says. It is a weird thing to say, but the man's mother says it anyway. It is true, of course. The man and woman will not, not in this timeline or any other that will ripple out from here. They will exist in this moment only, they will never time travel or board a ship. Despite this, they will be some of the happiest people in Earth's final decades because they have each other.

"The news said the wall of water was dozens of feet tall! Hundreds dead, they think it will be thousands!" the woman says, repeating the news.

"Hmm mmm," the man says again. He is staring at the screen as CNN shows the same footage over and over again.

Tsunami. Indian Ocean. May be the worst natural disaster in the history of the modern world. Someone, a scientist of sorts, is talking with the host of the show.

"This was a 9.1 magnitude earthquake," she, the scientist, tells the journalist.

The man has no idea what "9.1" means, but the way the scientist talks, it sounds big. He wonders how big an earthquake would need to be to rip the Earth apart?

And then there is the footage. The destruction. It took days to fully understand how bad it was as television crews had to go to the area. Pretty much everyone in the path of the water was wiped out, including any ability to report the damage.

The scientist is explaining more. Talking about "end of world" events like this. She means in the sense of a person's world. Like a neighborhood, or nation. The world less as a planet, and more as the meaningful thing we know.

The man can't help but think of his grandparents. They are "bible thumpers." Fire and brimstone types. They are convinced they will be raptured any day now. They are as convinced of this as much as they know he will regret not having children.

"I just wish we could do something to help them," the woman says. This is a common refrain from her. She is a good person. She always wants to help. In the coming shifts of the timeline, she will be a number of different helpers. In this one, she will continue to be a teacher though.

Although the man has not done so in years, he prays to God silently. It's more meditation, but he thinks it still counts. As he stands up, he accidentally knocks over his drink on the coffee table.

"Ah, shit!" he says. "No, I'll get it," he says gesturing for her to stay seated.

He goes to the kitchen and pulls at the paper towels above the sink.

He does not know it, but earlier that day a spider, tired and looking for a place to rest, thought the soft towels would be an ideal place for her to leave her sack of eggs. White, like cotton, they blend perfectly with their surroundings. The window, too, is ideal to catch prey which her children will need soon.

As the man draws the paper towels down, and bunches them in his hand, he crushes the spider's eggs. Then, walking back to the living room, he drowns the remains in the remnants of his spilt drink.

The spider bereft on the window prays to her goddess to intervene.

The prayer is answered. God has just come from spending lifetimes with the Centapedials.

God appears as the goddess of all spiders—massive, glittering with the subtle geometry of divinity. An arachnid presence. Eight legs, eyes without number.

"Help me," the spider mother says. "Save them."

God peers down at the crumpled nest, the damp towel, the man watching television. "Ah. Yes. I see." Her voice is less a tone, and more frequency carried through silk. "That is... unfortunate."

"You're the Goddess," says the spider. "Do something!"

"I saw the wave coming," God says quietly. "The earthquake. The pressure building in the plates beneath the sea. That was days ago."

"I don't mean the wave and those monstrous humans," the mother spider says. "I mean my children."

God sighs as spiders do. Her legs twitch on a taut web, her eyes cloud.

"Yes. Well. I know your people believe in the Weaver of Worlds, the one who spun the stars and caught the dead in her Web. And there is some truth to that. But I'm not a rescuer, little one. I'm... well, that's not really how it works."

The mother spider is silent. The web vibrates with disbelief.

"If you won't save the innocent," she asks, "then what is the point of you?"

God tilts her shimmering body, regarding the kitchen, the man, the towels, the couple on the couch.

"Sometimes," the Goddess Spider says, "the point is just to be here. To keep listening."

The mother spider stutters the way spiders do. She pricks at the web in agitation. Her body still aches with the weight of lost children.

God stays a moment longer.

"I mean, if you wanted, of course, we could just have a conversation..."

ACKNOWLEDGEMENTS

This collection owes its existence to many people's encouragement over many years. I first began writing these stories (*Waiting Room, Two by Two,* and *Leg Up*) while a community teacher in Dayton, Ohio. I was fresh out of undergraduate studies and contemplating whether to go to graduate school. I eventually took the plunge, and for the next six years of college, coupled with six more as a new faculty member, stole moments here and there between researching and teaching to work on this emerging world that mirrored ours but was not quite us.

I owe special thanks to the award committee of the Antioch Writers' Workshop who generously chose *Waiting Room* for a prize and provided a scholarship for me to attend their fiction writing classes in Yellow Springs, Ohio. The feedback I received from the teachers and fellow writers pushed me to keep working on this project. Likewise, I owe thanks to the editors of *TERSE.*, *Rag Queen Periodical*, *Dayton Daily News*, *Flights*, and the *Washington Pastime Review* for publishing earlier versions of some of these stories.

I also want to thank my good friends and colleagues Ricardo Quintana-Vallejo, Marc Valle, Lindsay Holman, Leslie Worthington, and Chris Heisserer for reading multiple versions of these stories as I began to edit them for this collection.

Finally, I dedicate this collection to Allison, my first reader and best friend.

ABOUT THE AUTHOR

Wesley R. Bishop is an assistant professor of American and Public history at Jacksonville State University in Alabama. His books have included *COVID-19 Haiku*, *Digital Self: Poems and Illustrations*, *The Long March of Coxey's Army*, *The Sound of Color*, and *Liberating Fat Bodies* (co-authored with Bessie Rigakos). He is the founding and managing editor of North Meridian Press.

ABOUT THE PUBLISHING TEAM

Nate Ragolia is a lifelong lover of science fiction and its power to imagine worlds more hopeful and inclusive than the real one. His first book, *There You Feel Free*, was published by 1888's Black Hill Press in 2015. Spaceboy Books reissued it in 2021. He's also the author of *The Retroactivist* (2017). His most recent book, *One Person Can't Make a Difference* (2022), was featured on Tor.com's Can't Miss Indie Press Speculative Fiction list, and was translated into Italian for Ringworld Sci-Fi in 2023. He founded and edited *BONED*, a literary magazine, and also created two webcomics. Nate is also a husband and a dog dad.

Shaunn Grulkowski has been compared to Warren Ellis and Phillip K. Dick and was once described as what a baby conceived by Kurt Vonnegut and Margaret Atwood would turn out to be. He's at least the fifth best Slavic-Latino-American sci-fi writer in the Baltimore metro area. He's the author *Retcontinuum*, and the editor of *A Stalled Ox* and *The Goldfish* for 1888/Black Hill Press.

www.ingramcontent.com/pod-product-compliance
Lightning Source LLC
LaVergne TN
LVHW040053080526
838202LV00045B/3620